MOON DAUGHTER'S FATE

AUTHOR:
Alice Peng

EDITORS:
Jeff Harkness, Matt Finch

SUBSTANTIVE EDITOR:
Brandon Powers

SWORDS & WIZARDRY CONVERSION:
Jeff Harkness

ART DIRECTOR:
Casey Christofferson

LAYOUT:
Suzy Moseby

INTERIOR ART:
Santa Norvaisaite, Adrian Landeros

CARTOGRAPHY:
Robert Altbauer

FRONT COVER ART:
Michael Syrigos

COVER DESIGN:
Casey Christofferson

NECROMANCER
Games™

NECROMANCER Games
ISBN: 978-1-6656-0021-7
SW PoD

Table of Contents

MOON DAUGHTER'S FATE

By Alice Peng

A Swords & Wizardry adventure for for 4–6 characters of 5th – 7th level

Chapter One: Introduction

This adventure by Alice Peng is suitable for 4–6 characters of 5th to 7th level, and is located in a fictional, folkloric region of China. If the gaming group is using existing characters, the means by which they reach the Whisper Valley is best determined by the context of their prior adventures.

Overview

The setup for this adventure begins with the characters discovering a provincial roadhouse where a terrible attack occurred, during which a young woman was taken. The situation is, however, one of considerable significance. A powerful deity of the region was trapped during the battle and still lingers in a state of poison-induced madness. The characters must track down the missing woman and help restore the balance to the land before an evil cult (and the force behind their power) can cause widespread devastation.

Because the land's balance has been thrown off, another deity, Leigong (God of Thunder, Smiter of Evil) has become involved and identified the characters as a possible solution to the existing problem. Their encounter with Leigong marks the beginning of the adventure.

Reading the Adventure

The first appearance of each name in this adventure contains a guide to its tonal pronunciation.

The pronunciation of a syllable is designated with a number: 1, 2, 3, 4, or none.

1: A high tone, a tone used in English when someone sounds surprised.

2: Goes from down to up and sounds a bit like a question mark would follow it.

3: Goes from down to up. Rather than sounding like a question mark, this is a more extended syllable.

4: Goes from up to down. Sometimes it can sound like someone's adding an exclamation point to their word or sound almost a little angry.

No number is a common sentence ender with no true equivalent in English. The word is pronounced extremely quickly and drops in the second half of the syllable.

Adventure Start

The adventure begins when the characters encounter the disguised god *Lei²Gong¹* (Leigong) on the road to the city of *Wei⁴Feng¹* (Weifeng, "Reason's Wind"), and they are most likely diverted from the main road to a smaller, more rural route. It is relatively clear from the encounter with Leigong that an adventure lies along the rural path, and the characters have no pressing business in Weifeng. While there are clues in Leigong's appearance to his identity, the characters will only know him as an old man.

Mandates of Heaven

The mandates and rules of Heaven outline acceptable actions for gods meddling and interacting with the world of mortals. This often prevents gods from taking direct action unless within a specific domain.

For example, Leigong can punish someone by striking them down with lightning but his lightning can't penetrate into many locations so he must use mortals to handle the situation.

Leigong is a Chinese Taoist deity known as the "Duke of Thunder" or "Thunder God." Heaven mandated him to punish mortals and spirits alike that used their knowledge of Taoism to commit evil acts. His deific depictions often have him with claws, bat or red-feathered wings, an axe or hammer, a chisel, and a set of drums.

The Encounter with Leigong

Read or summarize the following information to the players, adding whatever transition you feel is necessary from their prior adventures:

The province of *Sheng¹Xi¹Gu³* (Sheng Xi Gu, "Whisper Valley") is flanked by two high mountains to the northwest and southeast, and bounded by hills to the northeast and southwest with the *Bi⁴Jiang¹* (Bi Jiang, "Silk River") flowing through. Abundant in agriculture, coal, and trade, Shen Xi Gu is a wealthy and metropolitan province with major trade routes passing through the hills bounding the ends of the province.

You are traveling to the metropolitan city of Weifeng over hilly country for the late-summer *Qi¹xi¹* (Qixi, "The Night of Sevens") holiday festivities. You are not pursuing any mission in particular, but you are looking forward to the festival.

Along the road, however, you run into a strange encounter.

Any character with some kind of divine attunement can get a sense that the man might be more than he appears to be. Characters knowledgeable in religion can connect the symbolism in his winged robe and axe to Leigong but should not be able to make any overt connections.

Read or summarize the following information to the players.

> As you travel down the road, you begin hearing a rhythmic sound reminiscent of thunder but not as loud. It is definitely not thunder, though, since there are no storm clouds in the sky. The source of the noise turns out to be an old man dressed in a red-winged robe, chopping wood with an axe. Each time the axe falls, it creates the thunder-like noise.

This is the god Leigong in human guise. He pretends to be a simple man cutting firewood and introduces himself as *Lei²Lao³Ye* (Old Man Lei — *Lei²* can be interpreted as simply a common surname but that same word also happens to mean Thunder). Leigong is manipulating weather and terrain in the hopes that the characters' natures will be inclined to go where Leigong is unable to.

Assuming that the characters engage him in conversation, he informs them that the road ahead is washed out, and that if they are on their way to Weifeng, they might be delayed if they plan to arrive in time for the Qixi festivities. He does, however, tell them that they already passed another way to the city only half a mile back. It is longer, but now that the main road is washed out, it is probably still the quicker path. It is also, he says rather enigmatically, the "better" path.

The characters can continue to talk with Leigong, but the mandates and rules of Heaven (see the **Mandates of Heaven** sidebar) prevent him from giving them any further useful information. The only other thing he says if asked for further information, and it is of as-yet-unknown significance is: "Well, I'm chopping wood, you are on the road to Weifeng, and the price of coal seems to be going up in Mei Zhen." If the characters ask about Mei Zhen, he tells them that it's a coal-mining town that can be reached on the smaller turn-off behind them. Beyond this, he gives them no further information, saying that he has to get back to his work.

BACKGROUND

Nearly two decades ago, *Qing²Shan¹* (Qing Shan, "Passionate Mountain") fled execution for becoming pregnant before marriage. Fearing to be caught, she avoided cities and towns, but a group of bandits attacked her on the road, leaving her for dead. A traveling monk discovered her and brought her back to the provincial roadhouse he managed, where he witnessed the birth of Qing Shan's daughter, *Hua⁴Yue⁴* (Hua Yue, "Tranquil Moon"). After the monk died, Qing Shan has been the caretaker of the roadhouse with the assistance of her daughter.

Bandits in the area left the two women alone due to superstitions surrounding ill fortune and destitution falling upon anyone who violated the sanctuary of a provincial roadhouse.

Hua Yue grew up to be a musical prodigy and a lover of art. Visitors to the roadhouse have provided Qing Shan with all the necessary resources to raise Hua Yue with a proper education, even allowing Hua Yue to amass a collection of musical instruments — although most of these are of simple craftsmanship.

Niu²Tian¹Shen² (Niu Tian Shen, "Ox Lord of New Day's Toil"), the tutelary deity of the local region, receives his power from the sun and sows the fields. Several years ago, he was exploring his domain in human form when the gentle strains of Hua Yue's music mesmerized him. He started spending time at the provincial roadhouse regularly, always visiting in his human guise. Over time, he fell in love with the beautiful young Hua Yue.

Niu Tian Shen hid his true nature from Qing Shan and Hua Yue, leading them to believe he was just a traveling chronicler named Niu, but he secretly used his favor to help the roadhouse prosper. The gardens grew more bountiful, fewer vermin found their way onto the property, and the buildings seldom needed repair. The roadhouse was blessed with good fortune that had been unseen for generations. With each visit, Hua Yue found herself more enamored with the odd, massive man and eventually developed feelings of her own for him.

Niu Tian Shen's wife, *Mei³Lan²* (Mei Lan, "Beautiful Orchid"), a fairy, discovered that the man she loved and obsessed over was enamored with a mortal. Mei Lan decided in her rage that if her husband was going to love a human, that humans would be his undoing. Jealous and angry, she cast a spell into the seeds of a flower that she cast into the wind. The seeds' objective was to seek out a woman with greed, anger, and pain consuming her heart … and plant themselves within her. Of course, being "the doting, loving, and forgiving wife" that she is, she planned to use her *Shen²Xian¹* (Taoist Immortal Fairy) powers to save her husband in the end, if he'd only see the error of his bullheaded ways.

The seed cast onto the wind by Mei Lan found a woman named *Fei¹Du²* (Fei Du, Flight and Study). Fei Du had been sold to her husband at a young age, badly treated, then discarded by him in favor of a mistress. While conventional religions taught Fei Du that she needed to work hard on herself and that she would be rewarded through lifetimes of reincarnation, she was impatient. Instead, she sought to become a *shen²* (see the **Monsters in Chinese Folklore** sidebar at the end of the chapter for an explanation of shen) through moral shortcuts and evil acts, not knowing — or not caring — that it would corrupt and twist her essence into something else.

Fei Du studied legends and lore about those who gained power through supernatural means, scouring the lands and making deals in the dark. This ultimately led her to the discovery of a *soul gourd* hidden in the northern mountains, an item that once belonged to a vanquished immortal.

She experimented with the *soul gourd,* trapping people's souls and drinking them to extend her youth. She also discovered that great — but fleeting — power coursed through her veins after she drank.

Fei Du amassed followers and now presents herself as a savior to those who have suffered significant loss and spiraled into self-destructive patterns. She promises them the power to shape their own fates — possibly even to bring back what they have lost. She even shares small sips of her draught with the most devoted of her followers, empowering them to do her bidding.

Led to Fei Du by the seeds implanted in her, Mei Lan approached the cult leader and laid out a proposition. In exchange for Fei Du's and her cult's service, she would grant Fei Du's desire for everlasting power. As proof, Mei Lan provided Fei Du the means to capture and drink the souls of spirits in addition to those of humans. Intoxicated by this new power, Fei Du swore fealty to Mei Lan, not knowing she was merely a means to the fairy's ends.

Mei Lan convinced Fei Du to set her sights higher, on more powerful gods. She seeded the idea of taking the essence of Niu Tian Shen without ever specifically suggesting it. When Fei Du asked her patron for aid in capturing Niu Tian Shen, Mei Lan was more than happy to provide poison from a rare bird, the *Zhen⁴Niao³* (zhenniao, a daemon bird) to weaken the god. Armed with what she believed to be a foolproof plan, Fei Du sent a contingent of her most loyal followers to the provincial roadhouse to set her trap. This brings us to the present day.

The cultists arrived at the provincial roadhouse in the guise of weary merchants making their way to the Qixi Festival to sell their goods.

Note: Cultists are referred to using the masculine pronoun for ease of reading and writing. Given the coed nature of the cults, these unnamed cultists may be of either gender.

Armed with hidden weapons and poison, the cultists spent the night lying in wait to ambush Niu Tian Shen in the morning.

Niu Tian Shen, however, did not visit the next day, and so the cultists released the ox that pulled their cart and feigned that it had broken loose. They then pretended to search for the ox to no avail so they could spend a second night at the roadhouse.

Again, Niu Tian Shen did not appear the following morning either. So the cultists told Qing Shan that they would simply take turns pushing the cart until they could find a farm from which to purchase or borrow an ox. They went outside and started to push, but secretly used their blades to break the wagon wheel.

They then told Qing Shan that they'd been too hard on the cart, which caused it to catch in the road and break. The cultists spent yet a third night at the roadhouse.

The following morning, Niu Tian Shen arrived. Quickly, the cultists went into action. While the two caretakers of the roadhouse worked to put breakfast on the table for all the guests, one of the cultists sneaked to their cart and retrieved a bundle of blessed swords from a hidden compartment. Another cultist planted vials of poison around the tree in the courtyard.

Others loaded *zhenniao poison* darts into their sleeve dart guns and waited for the signal to strike.

Unfortunately, one of the cultists became nervous, and jumped into action before the signal. He attacked Qing Shan in the kitchen but she screamed, alerting everyone. She bolted for the dining room but her assailant caught her and thrust a knife through her back before she stepped through the open doorway. The overeager cultist slit her throat as a display of power before tossing her body aside to join the fight.

The attackers, however, had deeply underestimated the power of the god they were trifling with, for even in human form, Niu Tian Shen's mass and prowess were formidable. The combat quickly turned against the cultists. In a blur, the disguised Niu Tian Shen overpowered the cultists. Unable to complete their objective, the surviving cultists still managed to take Hua Yue hostage, whereupon they fled.

Niu Tian Shen intended to pursue, but he needed to gather his strength and heal his wounds, so he stumbled to the tree in the courtyard, one of the anchor points in the region, to borrow its lifeforce. When his hands touched the poisoned tree, he fell unconscious and lost his corporeal form.

Since then, Niu Tian Shen has been bound within the magically envenomed circle around the tree. Unable to flee elsewhere for healing, he has had two days to succumb to the poison and has devolved into madness.

MONSTERS IN CHINESE FOLKLORE

Daemons, spirits, and shen all refer to gods, of which there are thousands in the mythology. The same written word is used to describe soul, spirit, mysterious, supernatural, and beings of immense power. It is important to remember that in the mythos, a daemon or spirit isn't inherently good, evil, or neutral. Even two of the same type could have opposite natures or mixed natures. Two snake spirits could have wildly different views. One could believe in sucking the blood of humans while another could believe in the benevolence of Guan Yin's teachings.

Mogui (mogwai) comes from "mo" meaning evil beings that mean mortals harm, and "gui" meaning deceased vengeful spirits. There are many forms of these creatures that equate to modern translations as devils, demons, and undead.

Chinese fairies come from the story of the Eight Fairies. It talks about how humans ascended to immortality, gaining the status of shen through esoteric Taoist disciplines. Exact powers of these immortals tend to vary depending on the story, but generally include teleportation, martial prowess, cunning, deception, and social manipulation. The nature and behavior of the fairies have a lot in common with the fairies of the Western world.

CHAPTER TWO: THE PROVINCIAL ROADHOUSE

The adventurers arrive on the third day after the attack on the roadhouse.

START

Some of the characters may have information involving the local animals and vegetation that precedes their arrival at the provincial roadhouse. Druids, rangers, and wilderness-oriented characters notice that the wildlife has quieted or become absent during the last two days of the party's travels. Last night, even the song of crickets did not accompany the characters when they camped under the sky.

Druids, elves, and rangers may also notice that the local flora has become especially dry and haggard over the past two days of travel, even for these summer months.

No die roll is required for the characters to notice the oddity of the area; it is automatically apparent to anyone attuned to nature. Once you have given out any of this information as needed, read or summarize the information below.

> You have been noticing storm clouds roll across the sky all day, and they have begun to rumble their discontent. You might have stopped earlier on the lonely road, in the poor cover of a few trees were it not for roadside markers that promised a roadhouse ahead. Unfortunately, the road proved to be longer than you expected, and by the time the building appears ahead, the rain has started in earnest.
>
> The building looks inviting, and the once dry, cracked road has quickly turned to a muddy track that only increases the desire for a clean dry bed inside. Heading toward the entrance, you pass an unattended cart only partially protected by a tarpaulin from the rain.

THE ROADHOUSE

If the characters investigate the cart more closely, they can learn a few things:

- The crates and jars are partially filled with sand and dirt, and there's nothing of value. This should immediately strike the characters as odd. While the crates and jars are labeled to contain trade goods such as tools, linen, and lanterns, an inspection of their contents reveals they are partially filled with only regular sand and dirt.
- One of the cart's wheels is damaged. Investigation reveals that the wheel seems to have been intentionally broken using a bladed weapon. Coal dust is caught in the impact marks.
- A dirt-covered (quickly turning to mud) yoke for an ox is shoved into the back of the cart, the straps on it broken. Investigation reveals the straps were intentionally cut.
- One small box up by the driver's seat is filled with straw and wood shavings. Further examination reveals indentations for several small pouches that were once housed here. The pouches appeared to be porous in nature and left a small amount of herbal residue in the box.
- A light dusting of coal is under the protected tarp.
- A heavy blanket cascades out of a concealed compartment underneath the cart. This is where the cultists smuggled their swords. The swords were retrieved in a hurry; the compartment was left unpacked because the cultists assumed a sure victory and time to pack it away properly.

A-1. FOYER/SHRINE

> You shake off the rain as you step into the dim room. The only source of light is from the fading light outside filtering through the heavy rain clouds. Unlit lanterns hang from the rafters above you, and the center of the room houses a cold drying stove. A shrine along the far wall features the smiling figurine of a bearded old man wearing an ox horn-shaped hat. To the figure's left, a vertical banner hangs with three *hanzi* (characters) proclaiming the figure's name to be Niu Tian Shen. A similar banner to the right features a poem expressing his spheres of influence as agriculture, growth of plants, health of wildlife, and that he "reigns after the rooster crows but rests before the afternoon light." The figure stands on a cloth-draped table featuring various plates of offerings arranged before him as well as a bowl of uncooked rice holding three sticks of spent incense.
>
> An open bundle of incense rests on a side table along with two lid-covered ceramic donation dishes. One is marked "House," and the other "Spirit." Several kneeling stools are set in front of the shrine, and a large woven rug sits askew on the floor.

The stove is empty and has not been used in some time. This is common during summer months. The food offerings on the altar have spoiled and rotted.

Inside the House dish, the characters find the canine tooth of an animal along with several coins yet to be collected. The Spirit dish has a tightly rolled ball of pungent herbs covered with paper along with a small sum of spirit money (see **Appendix B: New Items**). The tooth is from a tiger. The pungent herbs match the residue found in the box by the driver's seat of the cart outside.

The characters should understand a few things at this point:

- It is customary for someone to greet travelers who visit roadhouses. The characters have not received a proper welcome.
- They are expected to pay respects to the local god by lighting incense, kneeling, and bowing several times before resting the incense in the holder. A few prayers are traditionally recited at this time.
- Travelers who are able to do so are also expected to leave a small donation in the dishes: standard money in the "House" dish and spirit money or herb effigy in the "Spirit" dish for the god. People make offerings and donations upon arriving, and some make additional offerings when they leave.

The characters find no evidence of the attack in this room, because the attackers came to the roadhouse under the guise of being weary travelers and did not strike until they were already inside the compound.

If the characters show proper reverence through prayer while inside the shrine, Leigong grants them a boon. In game terms, the character can make single reroll during the course of the adventure. The character can take the better result of the two rolls.

Map A: The Provincial Roadhouse

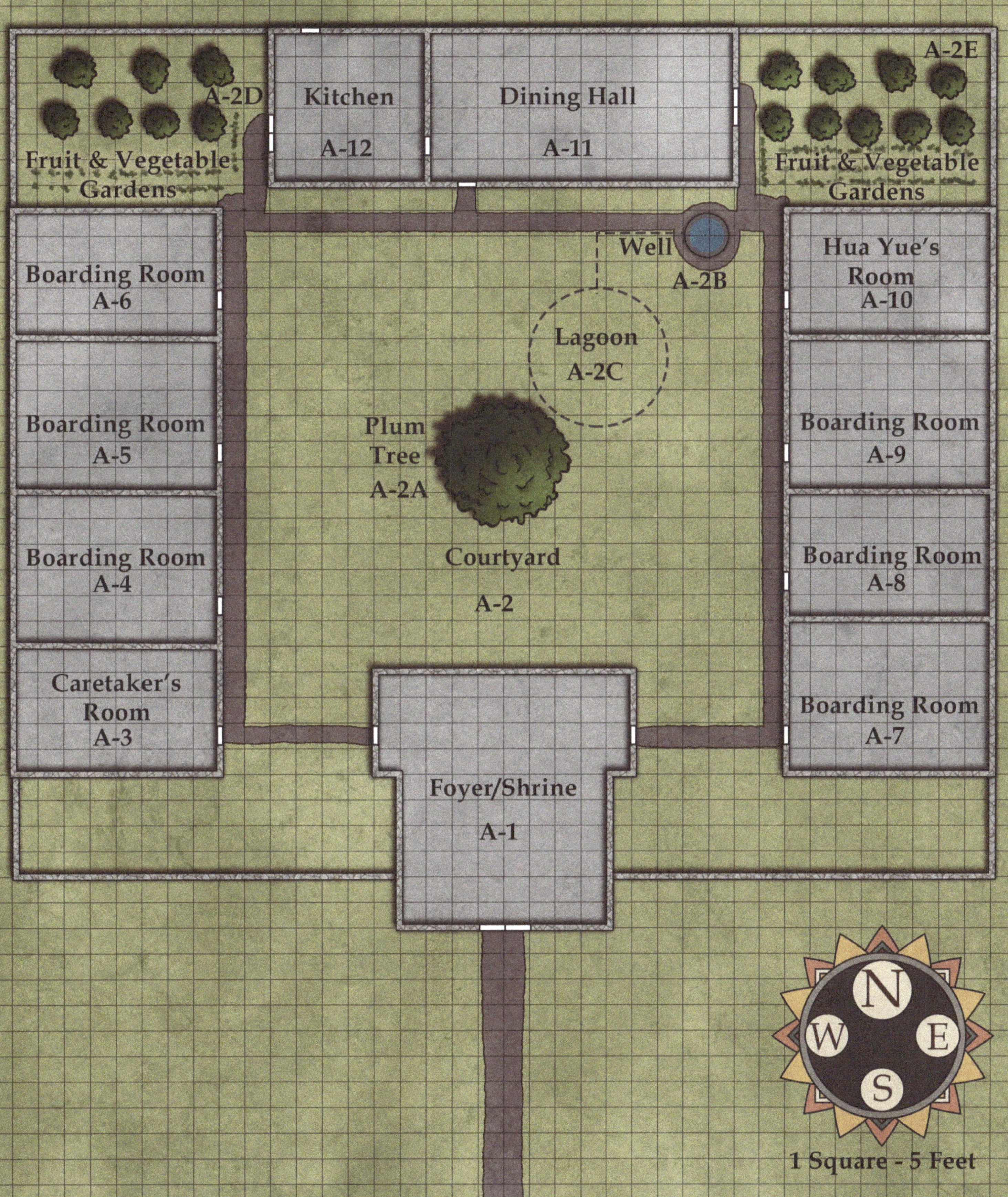

> You are looking out into a stone paved courtyard surrounded by the buildings of the roadhouse. The rain continues lashing down, and it is hot and muggy. Rain is unusual this time of year, and torrential rain like this is nearly unheard of. Your clothes immediately cling to you from a combination of your sweat and the rain blowing under eaves of the buildings.
>
> Several limestone benches are arranged around the courtyard along with one limestone table and five stools. What was once a magnificent plum tree with fruit still hanging from its branches stands in the center of the courtyard, but the entire tree is withered and rotting. A well is in the far corner of the courtyard near a doorway.

Characters investigating the courtyard notice blood in the courtyard that the rain is quickly washing away. Those who press their investigation despite the weather find traces of blood trails that can be tracked to two locations. One blood trail leads to the dining hall (**Area A-11**). Characters can determine that the blood trail started in the kitchen and traveled into the courtyard.

A2-A. The Plum Tree

The other blood trail leads to the plum tree in the center of the courtyard but then disappears. Characters have a 1-in-6 chance to determine that large humanoid footprints also end at the tree (3-in-6 for rangers, elves, and druids). They can also find a large indentation where a human fell onto the earth beside the tree before disappearing. Two large human handprints are burned into the tree trunk.

If the characters stay sheltered under the awning and investigate other rooms in the compound first, the blood is washed away by the time they investigate the courtyard.

Characters who approach the plum tree hear snorting and clomping sounds when they are 15 feet out. If the characters continue to press and cross the 10-foot mark, **Niu Tian Shen (incorporeal bull form)** steps out from the tree, and attacks.

Niu Tian Shen (Incorporeal Bull Form): HD 14; **HP** 105; **AC** −1[20]; **Atk** strike (3d8 + poison slobber); **Move** 15; **Save** 3; **AL** N; **CL/XP** 17/3500; **Special:** +1 or better magic weapons to hit, incorporeal (half damage from weapons), poison slobber (save or rot, 1d6 damage per round until washed off or healed). (see Appendix C: New Monsters)

Every time Niu Tian Shen takes damage, the tree mirrors his wounds. Fruits wither and rot, and leaves change color and fall as the tree breaks apart.

Each time he's forced to fight, characters hear the deep rumbling bellows and snorts of a bull in pain. If the characters engage this manifestation but then retreat, the manifestation cannot pursue due to being caged inside the dirt-covered area around the tree. Niu Tian Shen slams against an invisible barrier before vanishing.

Characters who attempt to communicate with Niu Tian Shen have to calm him, either through natural skill and talent or by playing music. Any characters skilled in musical instruments but who don't have one with them may find something suitable in Hua Yue's room (**Area A-10**). Hua Yue's xiao is exceptionally effective at calming him. Characters who roll below their dexterity on 4d6 can play an instrument well enough to calm Niu Tian Shen.

If the characters are able to calm the manifestation, communication is still limited due to Niu Tian Shen's mental state — but they can get a few words such as "attacked," "poison," "monsters," and "love" between bellows, low growls, and snorts. Feel free to add garbled gibberish between the recognizable words.

There is a way to improve the god's condition, but it requires giving him a potion (see the **Yang's Potion** sidebar), which is not possible unless he manifests in corporeal form. Once the poison is removed from the tree, which happens one way or another (see the **After Nightfall** section), Niu Tian Shen materializes in corporeal form in the hills to the northeast of the roadhouse at sunrise. If the characters rescued the dragon Yang and talked with him, they may be in time to meet the god when he materializes in corporeal form, give him the potion, and bring him back to the dragon for additional help.

Freshly dug earth can be found about 10 feet out from the trunk. If Niu Tian Shen's incorporeal form is calmed, defeated, or distracted by combat with other members of the party, characters investigating the upturned soil find five empty pouches planted equidistant in a ring around the tree.

The five empty pouches housed some sort of poison that disseminated into the earth around the tree. Each pouch contains remnants of one of the five elements planted in order around the tree: wood, fire, earth, metal, and water. The exterior of each pouch is marked with each element's hanzi written with smeared coal powder.

Clerics or other characters with a divine background can determine that these pouches are used to poison a shen's bond with their domain. With time, they can also identify some of the components as fairy spit and a variety of herbs, and that the ingredients were combined with magic.

Assassins and characters familiar with poisons recognize the zhenniao feather barbs and spines packed into each pouch.

A-2B. The Well

This appears to be a normal well. The taut rope hanging from it indicates a bucket at the bottom. A quick glance shows the bucket appears intact.

> The water ripples from the heavy rain splashing against it but the water looks fresh and clean. Bits of light glint against the bottom of the bucket from what appear to be large fish scales about three inches in diameter.

The scales are genuine silver and pearl, possibly from a silver water dragon, the spirits and guardians of large bodies of water.

The well water tastes metallic and smells like rotting vegetation, but it is safe to drink — for now. The smell is so slight that a bucket of water must be pulled up for the characters to notice it. The waterline appears to be about 50 feet down the well.

Vegetation growing on the inner wall of the well provides good handholds and makes climbing down easy (1-in-6 chance of falling for non-thief characters, and they can attempt a saving throw to catch themselves; on a failure they slip 1d6 feet and take the same amount of damage). Only one character can fit at a time into the diameter of the well. A character reaching midway down the well starts to hear faint echoes of speech (see the **Mei Gen** encounter below for the types of things that can be heard).

> As your feet touch the water, something slithers against one foot and reaches for your ankle. You scramble to ascend again but the rope-like vines growing against the well come to life and break apart. Boils of black ichor rise to the surface of each individual vine, making them look more like tentacles than plants. The ichor drips as they descend, attempting to wrap around you.

As soon as a character reaches the waterline, he or she is attacked by **4 canker vines**.

Canker Vines (4): HD 5; **HP** 36, 33, 31, 24; **AC** 5[14]; **Atk** slam (1d8 + entangle); **Move** 0 (immobile); **Save** 12; **AL** N; **CL/XP** 6/400; **Special:** acid (automatic 1d6 damage to entangled targets), entangle (save or held), sleep (entangled targets save or sleep as spell). (see **Appendix C: New Monsters**)

Once the characters defeat the canker vines, they are able to see more of the space at the bottom of the well.

> You can now see that the well taps into a slow-moving underground river. It is shallow enough for you to walk along the bottom while keeping your shoulders and head above water.
>
> A malicious cackle reverberates from downriver.

Following the cackle leads the characters to an underground lagoon.

> Rounding a turn in the passageway, you smell the immediate stench of fecundity and rot. Fungus of all shapes and sizes grow along the walls of a water-filled cavern, some giving off an eerie luminescent glow that is enough to see by. A silver-and-pearl-colored dragon lies on a tiny islet in the center of a large lagoon. Its blue beard hangs limply against the sand and grit. Tendrils from the same type of plant you fought minutes ago are wrapped along the coiled length of this magnificent creature.
>
> A pale, waiflike figure dressed in loose dark robes watches over the dragon. The figure has long warped fingernails, and veins bulge across its skin. It smiles with a venomous grin as it regards the helpless dragon. "Once my pet has had its fun …"

This mogui is *Mei² Gen¹* (Mei Gen, Rot Root). **Mei Gen** is clearly enraged at the interruption and exchanges haughty words with the characters before attacking to "dispose of the nuisance." If attacked, his eyes go black and green as lightning crackles from them. Listed below are some of the phrases he spouts at the characters; feel free to create your own based on these:
- "I didn't expect I'd get to have mortals for dessert so soon."
- "Leigong can't see so deep underground. What he can't see, he can't punish."
- "I'll feed your chi to my pets and make you into fertilizer."

Mei Gen, Rot and Fecundity Mogui: HD 10; HP 67; AC 2[17]; Atk 2 claws (1d8 + fungus rot); **Move** 12 (fly 12); **Save** 5; **AL** C; **CL/XP** 12/2000; **Special:** +1 or better magic weapons to hit, fungus rot (1d6 damage per hour, save each hour avoids damage, cure disease to end ongoing damage), spell-like ability, spores (10ft cloud, save or sleep as spell). (see Appendix C: New Monsters)
Spell-like ability: at will—lightning bolt (1d8 damage and fungus rot, save for half damage and avoid rot; if already affected by fungus rot, save or additional 1d4 damage and spores released).

If the characters defeat Mei Gen, the canker vines wrapped around the dragon *Yang²* (Yang, Ocean, Silver Coin) go limp and can easily be removed.

> The dragon stretches out with a yawn and jumps into the water. He swims around the islet for several laps, his tail splashing water onto the small land mass.

The **dragon Yang** is grateful for being rescued but rolls his eyes and feigns boredom if the characters become impatient trying to get his attention. Yang finally addresses the characters after a few laps. Yang is currently regenerating in the water. He is a little bit lazy but enjoys riddles and proverbs. In his mind, he always has time and many beings are just too impatient.

Yang, Very Old Wrath Dragon: HD 10; HP 60 (currently 31); **AC** 2[17]; **Atk** 2 claws (1d8), bite (2d12); **Move** 9 (fly 24); **Save** 5; **AL** L; **CL/XP** 17/3500; **Special:** breathes holy fire (90ft cone, 60 damage, save for half), polymorph self (at will), spells (2/2/1/1), turn undead (as 8th-level cleric). (see Appendix C: New Monsters)
Spells: 1st—cure light wounds, detect evil; 2nd—bless, hold person; 3rd—cure disease; 4th—neutralize poison.

> With a sigh, he tilts his head from side to side and steps onto the islet. His dragon body melts away and in its place is a human man dressed in diaphanous blue and white flowing robes, floor length pearlescent white hair, silver eyes, and blue lips. He straightens his clothes, dusts, and smooths out his sleeves.

Yang thanks the characters and introduces himself. The characters may have varying degrees of information depending upon how much of the roadhouse they have explored. After any initial pleasantries, the conversation most likely begins with the quote from the textbox below:

> Mei Gen, a mogui, came to my cave this morning after the big ox was attacked above. The mogui caught me while I was taking a nap. I can tell you this: He wouldn't have dared try such an attack on my lagoon if the ox was fully himself.

This is likely to cause the characters to ask questions about "the ox," and the conversation can proceed — approximately — along these lines. Depending on the questions the characters ask, not all of these points may get raised.

- The ox was attacked a couple of days ago.
- "The ox lives above but he also lives in the hills to the northeast. He comes to the place above often. He visits me sometimes, but he always wants something. It's always boring work that I don't want to do."
- Characters should get the impression that Yang finds Niu Tian Shen annoying and bothersome. Yang rolls his eyes, sighs, and shrugs a lot.
- "Ox comes in human form to visit the mortal girl above. She intoxicates him with her music, and he's enamored." Yang clearly disapproves of Niu Tian Shen's infatuation with the mortal.
- He mentions that the ox believes it is true love. If the characters press Yang about Niu Tian Shen's romantic life, the dragon may mention that the ox is rumored to be married to a fairy that lives high in the northwest mountains. Ox never goes into the mountains though.

Whenever it seems appropriate, Yang makes his request to the characters, roughly as follows:

> "Ox can't take human form now. He's in a state of madness and very sick. I can feel it seeping into the lands above, and it will soon reach my lagoon. If we don't help him, I may fall victim to it with time. You're clearly capable and understand the 'work, work, work' mentality. Will you help?"

If the characters ask what Yang means about "falling victim," he'll explain. "The ox is dying, and with him, the land. I have heard stories of deserts in distant lands where gods fought and died, but I have never seen it with my own eyes. I do not wish to see it."

If the characters agree to help, Yang pulls a small pearl vial from the sleeve of his robe. "Once you calm him, make him drink this. It suppresses the madness, temporarily, and should allow you to communicate with him."

Yang's Potion

The small pearl vial Yang gives to the characters is the only way to reduce Niu Tian Shen's madness to the point that the god can communicate relatively clearly, although it cannot restore him to full health. Once Niu Tian Shen drinks the contents of the vial, he remembers and is able to communicate as described in the **Memories of Niu Tian Shen** sidebar in Chapter Three.

If the characters demand payment, they obviously offend Yang. He reluctantly offers a handful of molted scales worth 2,000 gp but expects the characters to realize the error of their ways and decline. If any characters accept this payment, they are marked with his disfavor.

If the characters don't ask for payment, Yang remembers the characters and favors them in the future.

He encourages them to bring the ox to him because he believes he can diagnose the poison. It is possible he can design a cure if the characters help procure the rare ingredients.

Yang tells the characters that they should seek the ox out in the morning light on the pastures in the hills to the northeast. Touched by the rays of the sun, he should take the corporeal form of an oversized ox.

Yang provides the characters with very clear landmarks and says it should be a two to three hour walk for a human. It is important that they make it before high sun. He also warns the characters that the ox will not be in his right mind so they need to subdue or calm him.

If asked about music, Yang laughs and says, "Who is to say the ox wasn't mad before the poison? He did cut off his own horn and fashion it into a xiao (a vertical end-blown flute) for his mortal love. I'd never cut off my beautiful mane for anyone." He punctuates his statement by running a hand through his hair, pulling it forward over his shoulder. He then recites a proverb, "Those who hear not the music, think the dancers mad," and shrugs.

If presented with the coal pendants or the coal-covered sword with gelsemium on it (found in **Area A-7**), Yang pulls away, muttering a prayer, "Leigong protect me from such a fate." He is clearly scared and speaks in a hushed whisper about rumors of a dark cult that seeks power by taking the souls of daemons such as himself and the ox. He will also, if asked, explain who Leigong is (see the adventure start for details — Leigong is the disguised thunder god the characters met at the beginning of the adventure).

He can also give them the information that gelsemium is extremely poisonous to humans and many animals but has no effect on daemons, so it couldn't be what poisoned the ox.

"Several water sprites bring me fresh water from the mountains, and they tell me about the *Tan'shi* (Tanshi, coal addicts) working their waters, hiding underneath the mountains. The sprites say their leader is called Fragrant Poison. I think they are a dark cult seeking power and ascension through unnatural means."

"The water sprites say that the dark cult has caught a few of their number in the past but most of them are too fast and able to hide from the cultists."

A-2D. AND A-2E. FRUIT AND VEGETABLE GARDENS

These two areas cannot be seen or accessed from the main courtyard.

However, one peach tree in **Area A-2D** is worth noting:

These peaches are a gift to the characters from Leigong to reward and assist them. When eaten, they heal 1d6 + 4 hit points and allow the character to make saving throws vs. poison and disease with a +2 bonus for the next 24 hours.

The tree has four peaches. They remain ripe for 48 hours once picked from the tree, after which they rot and lose their healing properties.

A-3. CARETAKER'S ROOM

This is Qing Shan's room. Characters searching the room may find a small hiding space dug into the dirt under some floorboards by the bed. An old, dust-covered box rests inside and contains a wrapped martial arts manual titled *Day of the Seven Cranes* (see **Appendix B: New Items**).

A-4. THROUGH A-9. BOARDING ROOMS

These boarding rooms for travelers are all uniform and relatively sparse. The furniture is functional and serviceable but not new or expensive. Each room includes a nook-style bed, a table and two chairs, a tea set on the table, a ceramic latrine basin, and a mirror-less vanity with a large bowl and a pitcher.

Characters searching these rooms find a couple of travel satchels with basic travel necessities such as water gourds. A little coal dust is found on all of the satchels.

In the first two rooms the characters choose to investigate, they hear the chittering of rats nearby but won't find any to engage. The third room the characters investigate contains **1d4 rat swarms**.

Rat Swarms (1d4): HD 4; **AC** 7[12]; **Atk** bites (2d6 + disease); **Move** 12; **Save** 13; **AL** N; **CL/XP** 4/120; **Special:** disease (save or contract wasting disease, 1d4 damage per day until healed).

In **Area A-7**, the characters find a sword hidden in a travel-bedroll one of the cultists left behind. The weapon is in a poorly fitting sheath. Gelsemium flowers are engraved along the metal blade, which is also covered in coal dust. Assassins and thieves in the party may know that the coal dust is a trick assassins and some cults use so that their weapons don't catch the light. Characters versed in nature recall another name for these flowers: heartbreaker's grass. It is known to be an exceptionally poisonous yellow flowering plant.

A-10. HUA YUE'S ROOM

Two instruments stand out from the rest. A guqin, a seven-stringed zither, is decorated with inlaid coral shaped into a winged serpent. The other is a xiao, a vertical end-blown flute usually made of bamboo. This is *Hua Yue's xiao* (see **Appendix B: New Items**), which has a scene of a woman dancing her way to the mountains skillfully carved into the material. Closer inspection reveals that it is made from an animal horn and not the expected bamboo. The xiao detects as magical.

Hue Yue's xiao is made from the horn of Niu Tian Shen, who has a close spiritual connection to it. Given the strength of the connection and the pure nature of the xiao, Niu Tian Shen is able to burst the bonds holding him near the tree so he can defend the xiao from theft.

If characters remove the xiao from Hua Yue's room without playing it, **Niu Tian Shen (incorporeal form)** forms outside the room and attacks, trying to knock them back into the room (if the characters haven't already defeated him in the courtyard). The manifestation continues to attack the bearer of the xiao, gaining +2 to hit, damage, and saves against the character carrying the xiao.

The characters may manage to calm Niu Tian Shen by their diplomatic skills or by playing the xiao: see **Area A2-A**.

Niu Tian Shen (Incorporeal Bull Form): HD 14; **HP** 105; **AC** –1[20]; **Atk** strike (3d8 + poison slobber); **Move** 15; **Save** 3; **AL** N; **CL/XP** 17/3500; **Special:** +1 or better magic weapons to hit, incorporeal (half damage from weapons), poison slobber (save or rot, 1d6 damage per round until washed off or healed). (see Appendix C: New Monsters)

Searching the room uncovers a journal Hua Yue kept in her desk (or under her pillow). Flipping through it, characters find a few passages of interest:

I couldn't sleep again last night so I sneaked out under the moonlight and followed the stars. It was morning by the time I stopped on the hills in a beautiful pasture with spring flowers sprouting between the wild grass. From it, I can look down into the distance and see where I came from. The roadhouse is so small that I couldn't even pick it out in the distance.

I fell asleep in the grass. When I woke, a huge ox was standing still and staring at me. I was terrified at first, even screamed, but somehow the ox looked concerned for me and snorted several times.

When he didn't make a move toward me, I picked a handful of grass and offered it to him, then played music while he grazed beside me. I could have sworn he was dancing.

Journal Excerpt B

Mother says Master Niu sent word he'd be visiting tomorrow morning. I can't wait to play the xiao for him. It was such an extravagant gift; I can't imagine how much it cost. I wrote several songs for Master Niu. I'm so nervous. I hope he likes them.

Journal Excerpt C

I'm beginning to understand why mountains are the gateway to heaven. I brought a picnic to the hill today, my personal heaven. I made sure to bring some fruit in case the ox was there.

Oh, the horror! Poor ox lost a horn! I wish he could tell me what happened. I worry it hurts him. He ate the fruit from my hand and licked the juice off my arm. At least he's in good spirits despite missing one of his horns now.

Several other entries reference regular visits to the hill along with sketches of the area and the view from the hilltop. The characters can use these sketches and some basic knowledge to map their way to the location if they think of it.

In the entries, Hua Yue often mentions encountering Master Niu on the hilltop on a regular basis. She tends to detail those encounters with extreme care. Though she never comes out and writes it in her journal, there's a strong implication that Hua Yue has a significant crush on Master Niu.

Several other entries mention occasional encounters with the ox on the hilltop and the rapport the two built through music. She even comments on the absolute hilarity of watching the ox dance.

A-11. Dining Hall

Stepping into the dining hall, you come upon a horrific scene and the smell of death. What was once a rectangular wooden table and a dozen chairs is now a mess of broken and splintered wood. Three men and a woman are dead in this room, a couple of them draped over the broken furniture. Blades and sleeve dart guns lie just out of their grasps.

The corpses have begun to sprout a variety of fungi, mushrooms, and molds, with a large pool of blood producing a rainbow-colored growth. Their faces are obscured or decayed beyond recognition.

The door to the kitchen is closed, but you pick up the distinct scent of fresh steamed baozi, rice, and vegetables in the air mixing with the smell of rot and decay in the dining hall. Sounds of metal on metal can be heard from the kitchen.

A half dozen coal-dusted swords, two coal-dusted daggers, and two sleeve dart guns can be found scattered around the room. A number of the surviving attackers dropped their weapons as they fled with their hostage.

Characters familiar with the culture and practices of assassins note that covering a blade with coal or soot is a way assassins avoid having the blades reflect light and giving away their position.

The bodies of the men and women are dressed alike, with each wearing gray linen robes with white robes lining them. The only sign of wealth in their clothes is a red silk sash around their waist that mark them as poor merchants. All their clothes and the weapons found around this room have coal dust on them.

Investigating the bodies reveals that each one wears a pendant carved of chunks of coal. A seal is stamped onto each of them in red. The seals read "Duan Chan Cao" ("Heartbreaker Grass"). The bottom of each of these chunks of coal has been fashioned into a chop (a stamp most often used among the wealthy as their signature). Each chop has a different inscription.

Further investigation reveals that each body has several harnesses and scabbards designed to conceal a small weapon. One of them is also carrying a regional map with the roadhouse specifically marked on it (see **Map XXX**).

Characters investigating the corpses have a 1-in-3 chance of discovering and being attacked by **2d6 rot grubs**!

Rot Grubs (2d6): HD 1 hp; **HP** 1 each; **AC** 9[10]; **Atk** burrow; **Move** 1; **Save** 18; **AL** N; **CL/XP** 1/15; **Special:** burrows to heart (1d3 turns until death, 1d6 fire damage kills single grub, *cure disease* kills all grubs). (***Monstrosities*** 401)

A-12. Kitchen

The kitchen is bustling with activity. A middle-aged woman dressed in a floral robe soaked in blood stands over the stove with a wok in one hand and a metal spatula in the other. A stacked bamboo steamer nestled in another wok is over another section of the stove.

A closer look reveals that the woman's throat has been slit, her neck wound providing a gruesome second smile where the blood dried. Her disheveled hair is pulled up into a bun, but loose strands are matted with dried blood, gluing bits of it to her face and neck. A dagger runs through her from back to sternum.

In the lore, stories speak of people having their throats slit or tongues removed after death so the dead "can tell no tale (secrets)."

This is Qing Shan, who is now a **chi thief mogui**. She can talk with the characters but cannot provide any useful information because her attackers slit her throat so "she can tell no secrets" after they killed her. Her throat wasn't slit deep enough to render her mute, however. The slit throat acts as a curse on her.

The woman seems startled by your presence but turns to greet you. She attempts to smile, but the dead flesh on her face causes her face to contort strangely.

"Hello, hello! I trust my daughter has you settling in? Our humble roadhouse is getting quite full but I'm sure we'll find space to keep you all comfortable during your short stay! Go have a seat in the hall. Dinner's almost ready, and I made some baozi for you to travel with in the morning!"

Qing Shan is able to answer basic questions but does not remember the attack or details of her death:

- "I'm Qing Shan. My daughter and I keep this place running and travelers fed."
- "My daughter? Her name is Hua Yue. She's the one who greeted you when you arrived."
- "Three days ago, nine merchants arrived and suffered bad luck day after day so they stayed far longer than they expected. They weren't very sociable, so I mostly just let them be except for meals. (Her timing is off; it's actually been five days, because she stopped being able to track time when she died.)
- If the characters push Qing Shan to remember what happened, she'll explain things away with statements such as, "Oh, Hua Yue's probably run off to her hills again." Get creative if pressed for more.
- If the characters manage to find a way to force Qing Shan to confront her condition, she turns on the characters and attack. She loses what memories she does have until her next return.

Speak with the dead will not produce more information without first casting *remove curse* on her. Qing Shan's timing will be accurate if questioned under a *speak with the dead* spell, and she gives accurate accounts of the information she knows.

Qing Shan is a mogui but of a different subtype than Mei Gen. If the characters fight and defeat her, she rises again at moonrise and returns to maintain the grounds by sweeping the courtyard, watering the dying plants, picking dying plants to cook, and cooking in the kitchen. Each time she rises in this way, she is a more diminished version of her human self and becomes more easily angered and aggressive.

If the characters chop her into tiny bits, char her to dust, or make Qing Shan mush, she comes back without a body and is far more dangerous. Mogui without a body are prone to possessing those who do.

The only way to truly lay Qing Shan to rest is to have a suitable monk, cleric, or family member perform a transition ceremony that includes the burning of spirit money and special incense. A cleric can perform the ceremony.

Qinq Shan, Mogui, Chi Thief (Corporeal): HD 6; **HP** 41; **AC** 5[14]; **Atk** 2 claws (1d8 + level drain) or weapon (1d8); **Move** 12; **Save** 11; **AL** C; **CL/XP** 8/800; **Special:** +1 or better magic weapons to hit, level drain (1 level, save avoids), reform (return after 1d4 days). (See **Appendix C: New Monsters**)

A-13. Cellar

This cellar is little more than a five-foot-deep pit filled with varying sizes of ceramic jars. Some are used to store dry goods while others store fermenting foods. There's just enough space for one character to enter the pit and get to the stored foodstuffs.

Unfortunately, the accelerated corruption and rot which affects the roadhouse has already spread into this storage. About 50% of the containers of dried rice, seeds, nuts, and fruits are still edible, and 30% of the fermented products including dry and wet brined pickled peppers and various vegetables are still edible.

Characters find a silver *+1 short sword*, 6 *potions of healing* nestled in a box covered with sawdust and straw, and a spirit stone (a *luckstone*) stashed behind several fermentation jars on a shelf built into the wall. All of it looks rather old, untouched for quite some time.

The spirit stone is a piece of white jade shaped like a gourd with a red string and ornate knotting tied around it.

AFTER NIGHTFALL (UNFINISHED BUSINESS)

The rain stops around midnight but rumblings of thunder and occasional flashes of lightning ring in the distance well into midmorning.

Late in the night, if the characters haven't already pulled the poison satchels from around the tree in the courtyard, the rotting bark and bugs peel off the tree and shape into hands crawling around the courtyard searching for something. There are **4 fetid hand swarms** meandering around.

Some of these hands start digging at the dirt around the tree, tearing up roots and revealing the five buried pouches. Others crawl around the courtyard and possibly even make their way into rooms where the characters are spending the night. These hands crawl across the dark floor or drop out of the rafters. Characters are far more likely to smell them before they see them.

Fetid Hand Swarms (4): HD 5; HP 36, 32, 30, 28; **AC** 5[14]; **Atk** swarm (2d6 + curse); **Move** 12 (climb 12); **Save** 12; **AL** N; **CL/XP** 6/400; **Special:** curse (save or slow rot, 1d4 damage per hour until healed), nauseating smell (save or sickened for 10 minutes, −1 to hit and saves), resist edged weapons (50% damage), vulnerable to fire (200% damage). (see **Appendix C: New Monsters**)

After dealing with these hands, the characters find the poison pouches unearthed and displaced. Niu Tian Shen has been released and appears later in the hills.

An hour or two before dawn, if the characters haven't already explored the lagoon, they hear the sound of painful whimpers echoing up to the courtyard from the well.

Yang is far weaker if rescued at this time. He provides the same information as before but is far less playful about it, curling up in a ball on the islet in human form and on the edge of sleep during the entire conversation.

Chapter Three: The Northeast Hills

The Northeast Hills are approximately a two to three hour walk. Mention that the characters still hear the rumbling of distant thunderclaps during their journey despite it no longer raining or a cloud even appearing in the sky.

Niu Tian Shan appears on the hilltop at sunrise, and shortly thereafter a group of cultists arrive and attack him. Depending on when the characters arrive, they may have a chance to subdue and question the maddened god before the cultists come onto the scene.

> Even diminished by the poison you now know is festering in the land and its god, the hills northeast of the roadhouse are a place of beauty. Hiking up the hillsides, the grass grows taller, and you weave through copses of bamboo trees. What was likely green and verdant just a week ago now shows signs of drying and wilting. Leaves on some of the trees are wilting.
>
> White, yellow, and red wildflowers dot the landscape, many missing some or half of their petals. They reach for the sun along with the tall grass that stretches more than three feet high by the time you reach the hilltop.

Regardless of how things develop, the characters observe that whenever Niu Tian Shen exerts himself, the plants around him begin to die.

Arriving Before Sunrise

Characters who arrive before dawn are able to set up whatever procedures and precautions they would like while waiting for the ox's arrival. If they are looking for cover, the slope of the hillside and the tall grass are both options.

> As the sun crests over the mountains, you watch the hilltop for any signs of the ox. Sunlight catches on something you can't see, and it flares bright, momentarily blinding you. When your senses return, a massive ox with one horn and gashes in its shoulder and sides stands before you. It snorts, smelling the air, and clomps its hooves against the ground several times before backing away from your position and collapsing into the tall grass.

If Niu Tian Shen is calmed or subdued, the characters can use the draught Yang gave them to temporarily suppress his madness. Characters could also cast *neutralize poison* on Niu Tian Shen to make the draught's effect permanent and remove the poison, but it would require far more powerful magic than the characters have available to actually restore Niu Tian Shen to health.

A first, Niu Tian Shen is quite disoriented. Characters may need to pose questions, prompt him and fill in information they have gathered. Memories return in bits and pieces, but a complete picture can be formed by interacting with the characters.

Niu Tian Shen was looking in on his friends Matron Shan and her daughter, Hua Yue. Time hasn't been passing logically for him since he was poisoned, but with the characters filling in information, he guesses it happened four or five mornings ago.

He remembers the provincial roadhouse being filled with more guests than he'd seen in years, but not liking the smell of coal and filth that clung to the merchants gathering in the dining hall for breakfast. Matron Shan made porridge and fried dough with sweetened hot soy milk to drink. Thoughts of Matron Shan's food quickly distracts Niu Tian Shen. He rambles on about the various dishes she cooks and how they are all of the best quality.

He remembers Matron Shan screaming. He ran inside to help and was attacked. A moment later, a man emerged from the kitchen with Matron Shan's limp form shielding him. The assassin slit her throat before casting her aside.

Thinking back to before the fight, Niu Tian Shen recalls that one of the attackers might have slipped out to the cart parked outside and fetched larger bladed weapons. He saw a man bring a large, blanket-wrapped bundle in on his back but didn't think anything of it at the time.

After the fight, Niu Tian Shen recalls that he pulled himself to the plum tree, an anchor of his power. He hoped to re-energize himself with the divine essence imbued in the tree. However, when he pulled upon the energy within the tree, he discovered it was poisoned and corrupt. He can't remember or make sense of anything after that.

Everything after that is a haze, but he does remember someone calling out about orders "not to kill the girl." He had a panic attack when he realized he'd lost track of Hua Yue.

Unless he's captured and imprisoned by appropriate means, he remains anchored to this hilltop until he either heals or dies. Each morning, he returns to the hilltop as the sun crests the mountains.

He has other anchors across the region but this is the center of his power and where he is tied to most strongly. The nearest other tether is the poisoned plum tree in the roadhouse courtyard. But he is unable to return there due to the corruption ritual the cultists performed.

Unless the characters leave very shortly, they will be present when the cultists attack.

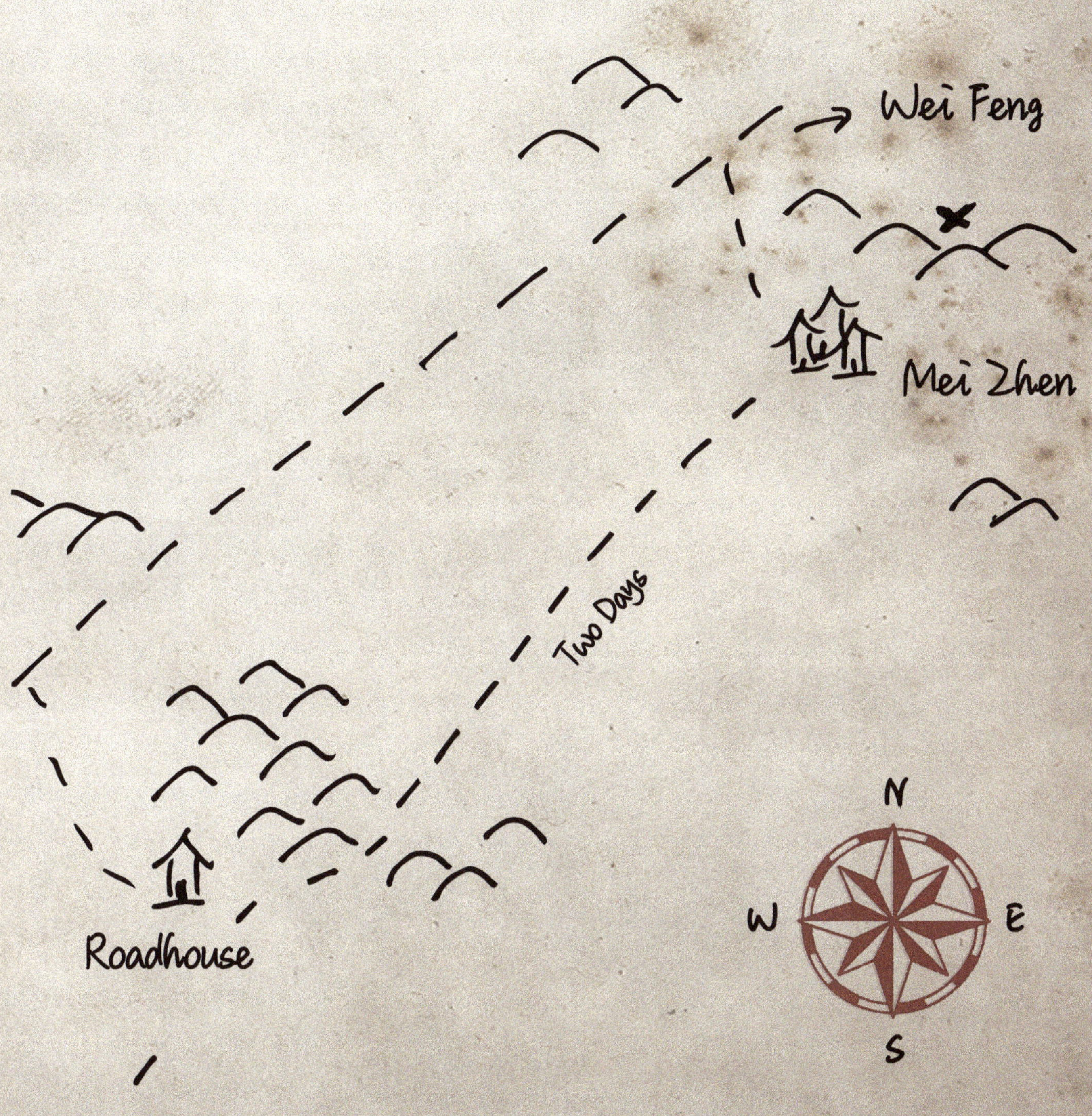

Cultist's Map

Arriving After Sunrise

Characters who arrive on the hilltop before high sun but after sunrise see cultists attacking Niu Tian Shen in his corporeal form of an unusually large ox.

The characters ascend the opposite side of the hill from the cultists, so they are unlikely to notice the cultists before the attack.

> Rounding a copse of bamboo trees, the sound of a loud bellowing animal rings through the air. Quickly searching for the source, you spot a massive, obviously wounded ox atop the hill. The ox is missing one of its horns and is fighting for its life against a handful of attackers.
>
> Neither side seems to notice your presence, allowing you to draw closer for a better look. Men and women are dressed in gray robes, red sashes, and wield coal-dusted blades that don't reflect the light. Each attacker's face has a hanzi (written character) drawn from forehead to chin, in black, likely coal dust mixed with water.

Niu Tian Shen will have little to no effect on a battle between the characters and the cultists, given his condition. The characters will have to defeat the cultists without any measurable help from the god. The battle involves a **cultist lieutenant**, a **cultist assassin**, a **cultist magic-user**, and a **cultist monk**.

Niu Tian Shen (Corporeal): HD 14; **HP** 105 (currently 45); **AC** 2[17]; **Atk** strike (3d8 + poison slobber); **Move** 15; **Save** 3; **AL** N; **CL/XP** 18/3800; **Special:** +1 or better magic weapons to hit, poison slobber (save or rot, 1d6 damage per round until washed off or healed), spell-like abilities.

Spell-like abilities: at will—detect evil, polymorph self, purify food and drink; 3/day—bless, cure disease, speak with animals; 1/day—neutralize poison, prayer.

Cultist Lieutenant, Male or Female Human (Ftr6): HP 41; **AC** 4[15]; **Atk** *+1 longsword* (1d8+2) or light crossbow (1d4+1); **Move** 12; **Save** 9; **AL** C; **CL/XP** 6/400; **Special:** multiple attacks (6) vs. creatures with 1 or fewer HD, +1 to hit and damage strength bonus.
Equipment: chainmail, shield, +1 longsword, light crossbow, 20 bolts, 2d6 gp.

Cultist Assassin, Male or Female Human (Asn6): HP 29; **AC** 6[13]; **Atk** short sword (1d6 + poison) or shortbow x2 (1d6 + poison); **Move** 12; **Save** 9 (+1, ring); **AL** C; **CL/XP** 6/400; **Special:** backstab (x3), disguise, poison use, thieving skills.
Thieving Skills: Climb 88%, Tasks/Traps 30%, Hear 4 in 6, Hide 25%, Silent 35%, Locks 25%.
Equipment: leather armor, short sword, shortbow, 20 arrows, *ring of protection +1*, zhenniao bird poison (save or die), 2d4 sp.

Cultist Magic-User, Male or Female Human (MU7): HP 23; **AC** 8[11] or 2[17] (missile) and 4[15] (melee) from *shield* spell; **Atk** dagger (1d4); **Move** 12; **Save** 8 (+1, cloak); **AL** C; **CL/XP** 7/600; **Special:** +2 save vs. spells, wands and staffs, spells (4/3/2/1).
Spells: 1st—*charm person, magic missile* (x2), *shield*; 2nd—*darkness 15ft radius, invisibility, phantasmal force*; 3rd—*fly, lightning bolt*; 4th—*wall of fire*.
Equipment: *cloak of protection +1*, dagger, *wand of paralyzing* (6 charges), *potion of extra healing*.

Cultist Monks, Male or Female Human (Mnk6): HP 22; **AC** 4[15]; **Atk** 2 strikes (1d12); **Move** 17; **Save** 10; **AL** C; **CL/XP** 7/600; **Special:** +2 save vs. paralysis and poison, +3 weapon bonus, alertness, deadly strike, deflect missiles, mastery of mind (90% chance mind reading fails), multiple weaponless attacks (x2), speak with animals, slow falling.

The cultists have a map showing a section of the region that includes the provincial roadhouse in the lower right corner and Mei Zhen on the upper left corner.

Questioning any captured cultists yields some information:

- The cultist is a devotee of Fragrant Poison, their great leader. She is so powerful that the goddess Mei Lan sought her out and promised her people a great future.
- The cultist doesn't fear death because they believe Mei Lan will reward them for their sacrifice.
- Becoming a cultist involved a ritual separation from the cultist's former life. They gave up property, name, and personal identity as a sacrifice to Fragrant Poison in preparation for true enlightenment. Every cultist is required to make this sacrifice.

Characters who develop a rapport with the cultist might make headway in reversing the brainwashing. Characters may be able to play on the cultist's previous identity to provide the fanatic some clarity and perspective. Doing so yields some better information:

- Their temple is located near Mei Zhen to the southeast. It is hidden deep below an abandoned mine.
- Fragrant Poison has a powerful magic item, but the cultist doesn't know the nature of its power.
- Characters need a key to enter the "great temple."
- Fragrant Poison and her followers used to operate out of abandoned houses in the recesses of the southern mountains until their new patron goddess moved them to the "great temple" a few months ago.
- Their new patron goddess created a magical doorway that the cultists use to enter the "great temple." The cultists wear chops around their necks; every supplicant must wear one to enter.
- This group was sent out when the provincial roadhouse attack failed.

Niu Tian Shen is scared and attacks at the slightest provocation, but he can be calmed by playing the xiao or by diplomatic skill. Characters who examine him after the battle with the cultists find barbs and broken shafts from zhenniao bird feathers in several of the wounds. Extracting them without doing more damage requires a healer's hands. Talking with the god after the cultist attack, provided he is calmed and given Yang's potion, yields the same information as if the characters had arrived before sunrise.

Returning to Yang

With the information the characters learn on the hill, they may choose to return to Yang with or without Niu Tian Shen, possibly hoping they can get him some help before the next morning light.

Read or summarize the following if the characters return to Yang during the day:

> Yang's serpentine form can be seen moving just beneath the surface of the water when you return to the lagoon. Sensing your presence in his water, he makes his way over and surfaces. He cocks his head from side to side scrutinizing you for several moments before changing into his human form. Despite being soaking wet, his robes float outward rather than cling to his skin.

Read or summarize the following if the characters return to Yang during the night:

> You return to find Yang's serpentine form coiled on the islet. He snores loudly, making small waves in the water with each exhale. The light shimmers against his skin, and you see the bruises from the canker vine pulse across his body. When you move into the water of the lagoon, he startles awake and leaps into the water. Moments later, he swims up to you, cocking his head from side to side. He scrutinizes you for several moments before changing into his human form. You see bruises on his arms, face, and neck. Despite being soaking wet, his robes float outward rather than cling to his skin.

If the characters didn't bring Niu Tian Shen with them, Yang is initially disappointed. He listens to what the characters learned, offering minimal feedback.

If the characters brought Niu Tian Shen with them, Yang pulls him deeper into the lagoon and attempts to heal him with the water and his powers. He encourages the characters to share what they've learned while he works.

Either way, Yang shakes his head in frustration when the characters finish catching him up on their progress and discoveries.

> "He is beyond my power but perhaps not beyond yours," Yang says. "I need answers. To get them, I need something that embodies the nature of a predator."

Yang emphasizes that it has to be something born of the beast such as a tooth, claw, feather, tuft of fur, or anything else that is suitable for dipping into ink. One possibility would be the tiger tooth the characters may have discovered in the foyer/shrine (**Area A-1**).

Characters can also offer items from their equipment that they feel fit this description if they give a good enough reason.

Adjust the following boxed text with the item and corresponding animal:

> Yang pulls a scroll case and vial of ink from his sleeves and settles down on his islet. He dips the (ITEM) you gave him into the ink and writes a series of characters vertically down the unfurling scroll. You hear a loud roar through the chamber, and the apparition of a massive (ANIMAL) blows through the room like a gust of wind. Carried on the wind, you hear, "To be made whole, body and soul, what was given freely must be returned with equal sincerity."

After due consideration and conversation with the characters, Yang will help the characters arrive at the conclusion that Niu Tian Shen's horn must be restored. Gifts are sacred and the horn was gifted to Hua Yue so she must be the one to return it sincerely and freely. This is why Mei Lan gave the cultists specific instructions not to harm the girl. She needs Hua Yue alive and well to control her husband when the horn is returned to him as part of her plan.

If the characters obtained the cultists' map and mention it to Yang, he asks to see it. When he has looked at it, he points out it is a map of the local region.

> "We're here. The hills are here. This, up here, is Mei Zhen, Coal Town," he points out.

Chapter Four: Mei Zhen (Coal Town)

By now, the characters should have enough information to realize that the coal mine near Mei Zhen is in some way associated with the goings-on at the roadhouse, and they will presumably head in that direction.

One Name, Different Meanings

Mei Zhen means "Coal Town," but can also be written to mean "Plum Flower Town" — it is still pronounced exactly the same in verbal communication. This confusion is frequent among people who aren't familiar with the area due to its reputation for being metropolitan and wealthy.

The characters must travel up a series of small roads and travel-beaten paths that take them northwest to Mei Zhen. The journey takes approximately two days. Along the way, the characters cross paths with miners, tradesman, and tourists during the latter half of the journey. The characters continue to hear distant thunderclaps during their trip, but these are relatively rare.

Gathering Information in Coal Town

When the characters arrive in Mei Zhen, the town's modest Qixi festivities are in full swing. They arrive on the third or fourth day of the seventh month depending on their travel plans. While not a metropolitan city like Weifeng, Mei Zhen receives its share of tourists due to its mistaken namesakes of "Plum Flower Town."

The locals aren't as jovial or festive as they are most years, given the recent troubles with people going missing in the mines, talks of people being cursed, and supplies going missing. They are generally putting on a brave face.

> Slow rhythmic thunder beats through Mei Zhen when you arrive, although it is not raining. Street stalls filled with food and wares line the way into the town square where the statue of a tree has been molded out of coal. Paper plum flowers are affixed to the branches in abundance.

The general flow of traffic leads the characters toward the town's square where an acrobatic troupe is performing around the tree. A man with a set of drums sits at the base of the tree, and the characters realize that the sound of thunder they have been hearing is actually the beating of this drum.

> Besides the slow rhythmic thunder of the red drum, the man's fingers are also tapping a quick and light rain sound. His long black hair has shocks of white playing in it, something you hadn't noticed during your first encounter. His booming laughter mixes into the music being played like a harmony synchronized with the melody. You quickly recognize the man's red-winged robes as the good samaritan who told you about the washed-out road a few days earlier.

Leigong

Once again, the old man is Leigong the Thunder God. Leigong introduces himself as Lei Lao Ye (Old Man Lei). Religious characters may recognize some odd similarities between Lei Lao Ye and stories of Leigong that they may have heard. Allow them to see resemblances but no outward assumptions.

He mentions that he recognizes the group but claims he can't quite place where they met before. When reminded, he laughs, "Oh, yes. My old addled mind. Come, you must be hungry. I know a little place with the best dumplings in the region!"

Lei Lao Ye is a larger-than-life drummer with a bit of a belly. When walking down the street with the characters, he alternates between drumming on his belly and the drum strapped to his side. He's a man of high spirits, and his presence easily fills up the room. He buys a round of drinks and meals for everyone in the establishment.

"So, did you get lost and turned around? Thought you all were heading to Weifeng? I hear the festivities there are pretty epic." If the characters share the reason for their visit to Mei Zhen, Lei Lao Ye mentions that there have been some rumors of troubles in the short time he's been in town but it's all very hush-hush.

He mentions that all the inns are full, but he's staying with some performers. They have a spare room the characters can share if they intend to spend the night.

Asking Around

The characters are able to move about town speaking with locals to learn some information. In general, people are welcoming despite being a little scared. They try to push characters into buying merchandise and items for the festival. Characters must build a little rapport with the townsfolk to loosen their tongues.

Goods for Sale

Itms being sold for the Qixi festival include carvings of exotic flowers, animals, and unusual birds. These are usually carved into melon skins but some dealers also offer carvings on wood and coal. A variety of teas, fruits, nuts, and melon seeds are being sold as offerings to the weaver fairy. Bundles of wildflowers are woven for hanging on oxen effigies, and fried pastries flavored for every fruit and flower can be found for indulging on. Qixi is also one of several holidays when skilled craftsmen travel to cities to peddle their services and wares. All the food is void of animal products.

Talking to Miners

A couple of miners gathered in tea and entertainment houses share stories for proper libations, vegetarian food, and good company.

The mining process involves digging a pit in the ground, setting up a pulley system up top much like a water well, and sending miners down with bamboo ladders to harvest while they tunnel.

In General

Most of the people in the area laugh off any talk of cultists, saying things such as, "Children's stories to make them behave," or "If coal-loving cultists exist, maybe I should join them. Do they have magical ways of mining that won't hurt my back?" or "Can the cultists regrow the leg I lost in a mining accident?"

The Elderly Miner

One elderly, superstitious miner tells the characters about a pit they abandoned after breaking through to the third level of Diyu (Hell), the Hell of Boiling Sands. It is a place where you burn in an ocean of hot sand and dirt. The sand itself comes alive to drag you into the smoldering heat and causes you to suffer eternal suffocation. He's very insistent that a number of young miners were pulled deep into the boiling sands by living sand. He tried to stop the search party but his warnings fell on deaf ears. When a handful of the search party returned, they were "as white as the dead." One went mad; the others packed up and left. The one who went mad is known as the "wrapped man."

The elderly miner or the wrapped man can give characters directions to the coal pit entrance to Nuwa's Fallen Palace (**Area B**).

The Wrapped Man

Characters can easily track down the maddened man who is known around town as *Lao Bao* (The Wrapped Man). He's is a panhandler who surrounds himself with red lanterns. He wraps his hat, shoes, and walking stick in strips of paper with calligraphy painted across it. The characters can immediately tell that those letters are attempts at *fu²lu⁴* (fulu, Taoist magic script).

Characters who understand the arcane or divine note that the fulu was not done properly and has no magical effect.

Lao Bao rants and rambles at anyone who will listen, "The dark ones, they came for my soul. They'll come for your soul." Characters who try to redirect or interrupt anger him. "You don't understand! They come in the night! They take us to feed their dark gods! Blood in the alleys. … Families from their beds …"

The Frightened Miner

Over drinks, a miner brings up that before they abandoned the cursed mine, he saw something strange one night. He left his tent to relieve himself and spotted a group of people all dressed in the same dark clothes. He leans in conspiratorially and adds, "It was a bright moon that night, not quite full but I saw they all had big hanzi drawn across their faces." He watched them approach a cliff where the earth folded in on itself to create a "V" in the wall. One by one, they disappeared into it. He peed his pants and took off back to town, leaving all his mining gear in the camp. "I ran all night …"

The frightened miner can give the characters directions that take them to the cultists' entrance to Nuwa's Fallen Palace (**Area B**). He will not accompany them to the place, however.

Talking to Townsfolk

The characters detect magical and fake fulu hanging from doorways and windows all around town. Inquiring about them with the owners of the homes and businesses reveals that the town has been suffering some bad luck in recent months.

People started going missing in the night three or four month ago. One at a time, a few days apart, and with no predictable pattern. It hasn't happened in about three weeks though.

Supplies also started to go missing regularly about four months ago. Expected shipments sometimes never arrived. There are no reports of banditry causing it, but people are worried there might be a food supply shortage if this continues.

Tools have been breaking unexpectedly, which causes some to whisper of the town being cursed.

Others instead argue that "Old Man *Fu²* (Fu, "charm/talisman") never cared for his tools," or "*Guan¹Po²* (Guan Po, "Matron Mountain Pass/To Close or Shut") bought the shovel from *Bai²Zhu²* (Baizhu, "White Candle"). Everyone knows he uses cheap materials and cuts corners. Of course it broke!"

Characters inquiring where people can learn that a holy man who lives in a small shrine to Leigong just outside town created them. People simply call him *Lao³Ye²* (Lao Ye, "Old Grandpa"); no one knows his real name.

Lao Ye

Lao Ye is a grizzled old retired monster hunter with scars across his face and body to prove it. He's willing to make each character up to two fulu if they make donations to the shrine worth at least 100 gp per character.

It takes roughly one hour to prepare himself to craft the fulu and an additional hour per fulu he makes.

Each fulu he makes wards the character from one saving throw during their encounter with Fei Du. This includes the poison tea. The characters may not even realize they were the targets of the save because the wards redirect the effects to the scroll.

Fulu Symbols

Fulu is a form of Taoist magic wherein symbols and incantations are written or painted on paper as charms, wards, and active spells. It stems from the ideas of words having power and, when written, the ephemeral becomes real. Several other Taoist aspects factor in also.

The Situation

Cultists are hiding among the civilians in Mei Zhen. They are participating in the festivities, selling goods as street vendors, and maybe even working as servers. Characters asking questions likely get their attention.

The cultists pay a street urchin to keep an eye on the characters. If the characters catch the street rat, he knows nothing about a cult and says he was just paid to keep an eye on the nosy tourists and report to a vendor selling coal-based artwork. Characters can pay the child more to point out the vendor who hired them. If the characters want to confront the coal-art vendor, remind them that they are in the midst of the Qixi festivities. There's a good crowd celebrating.

If they approach, the vendor's assistant intercepts the characters, asking if she can help them. The vendor uses this distraction to slip into the crowd and head toward a nearby residence. He's not trying to be particularly stealthy because he actually wants the characters to follow him. A large group of cultists is waiting to spring an ambush.

If the characters follow the vendor into the courtyard, **12 cultists** flood out of the buildings all around them while **4 dart blowers** pop up on the rooftops. They are led by **2 cultist monks**. The cultists on the ground flow out of the building in front of the characters, while two dart blowers are on each of the buildings to the left and right of the characters.

If the characters approach using stealth or some other method, they may be able to gather enough information to adjust the odds in their favor. If they are spotted, however, the cultists send up a firework to alert the others that something has gone wrong. The others converge on the area where the characters have been sighted.

Cultist Monks, Male or Female Humans (Mnk4) (2): HP 15, 13; **AC** 6[13]; **Atk** 2 strikes (1d8); **Move** 15; **Save** 12; **AL** C; **CL/XP** 5/240; **Special:** +2 save vs. paralysis and poison, +2 weapon bonus, alertness, deadly strike, deflect missiles, speak with animals. **Equipment:** coal chop (stamp)

Cultists, Male or Female Humans (12): HD 1; HP 6 each; **AC** 7[12]; **Atk** short sword (1d6); **Move** 12; **Save** 17; **AL** C; **CL/XP** 1/15; **Special:** none. (*Monstrosities* 254) **Equipment:** short sword.

Cultist Dart Blowers, Male or Female Humans (4): HD 1; HP 6 each; **AC** 7[12]; **Atk** blowgun (1d4 + poison); **Move** 12; **Save** 17; **AL** C; **CL/XP** 1/15; **Special:** none. (*Monstrosities* 254) **Equipment:** blowgun, 12 darts, zhenniao poison (save or die).

If questioned, any captured cultists reveal that a handful of fellow cultists are in Mei Zhen. They were sent away from the great temple a few days ago and ordered not to return until summoned. Many among them believe they are being punished for failing their leader and goddess.

See the description of the cultists in Chapter Three for other information they may know.

By the time the characters finish gathering the information, it is getting pretty late in the day. They may choose to accept Leigong's hospitality, in which case the night passes uneventfully. Or they may choose to get a head-start to their next destination.

Chapter Five: The Fallen Temple

Long ago, *Nu³Wa¹*, (Nuwa, mother goddess and creator of mankind), lived in a majestic palace built into the highest peaks of Heaven with her brother-husband *Fu²Xi¹* (Fuxi, the emperor god).

An ancient tale tells of a great war between two great powers of Heaven. The losing side was cast into the underworld and banned from Heaven. The fallout from this war and exile caused the Four Pillars of Heaven to crumble.

Nuwa combined her magic with the color-stones and raised Heaven back into the skies. But this selfless act came at the cost of being unable to save her own place of power. Nuwa's palace fell deep into the underworld, and with it, the remaining cache of color-stones she had painstakingly sought. The cataclysmic clash of powers placed everything in the palace and around it in temporal stasis.

CRYSTAL LEGENDS

According to legend and myth, Nuwa quested across the known worlds and gathered a cache of magical color-stones. These are believed to be akin to magical versions of crystals amethysts, azurites, quartz, jasper, obsidian, turquoise, etc. She smelted five of these magical crystals together to fix the Four Pillars of Heaven when they crumbled.

Mei Lan found a part of Nuwa's Fallen Palace by sheer luck and saw her opportunity to use its power. Wanting to keep a close eye on Fei Du and the disciples, she convinced the cult to upgrade from their abandoned farmhouses into the fallen palace.

When the cultists returned without Niu Tian Shen, Mei Lan took his blood from their weapons and sent the cultists away. She's harnessing the power of Nuwa's remaining cache of colored-stones to siphon her husband's lifeforce for her own ends. To ensure she wouldn't be disturbed, Mei Lan used her magic to awaken underworld energies and beings best left alone.

Fei Du didn't leave with the other cultists; instead, she locked herself in her room.

Only a small wing of Nuwa's Fallen Palace is accessible during this adventure. The remainder is buried or destroyed.

There are two entrances to the fallen palace, one through a coal pit and the other through a magic doorway used by the cultists. The characters can learn about either of these entrances from miners in Mei Zhen, and interrogating the cultists might lead directly to the cultists' entrance.

THE COAL PIT

If the characters investigate the coal pit mentioned by the elderly miner in Mei Zhen, they find signs hammered into the ground starting at about a quarter mile out. Most of the signs have no writing but are configured to warn of danger or cursed lands ahead. Unlit red lanterns hang off poles erected near the path to scare away evil. There's even a shrine to the ancestors and the dead on the town's side of the red lantern perimeter.

You find the abandoned mining pit surprisingly intact. The 15-foot-diameter pit's pulley system and rope are still attached at the top. With a quick glance down the hole, you see a small wooden landing wedged into the wall of the pit about 30 feet down. The remainder of the pit goes too deep for your eyes to see.

The characters must lower themselves a total of 300 feet before they hit bottom. They find a new wooden landing every 30 feet but each one is big enough only for one person to stand on at a time. The platforms have a 20% chance of breaking under characters carrying exceptionally heavy loads or who are wearing heavy armor. Characters who fall can attempt to grab the next platform down by rolling below their dexterity on 4d6. If they succeed, they halt their descent but take 2d6 points of damage. However, the new platform has a 40% chance of breaking under the sudden weight. It automatically breaks if someone else is already standing on it. Characters who fall from the final platform take 3d6 points of damage as they drop to the bottom of the shaft.

Occasionally, the characters discover small alcoves and other irregularities in the shaft, but none of these are full side passages or tunnels. Some are big enough for a character to stand or even sit inside if needed.

Once characters descend past 200 feet, **6 coal demons** pull themselves from the walls and attack.

The coal demons move just beneath the surface of the walls the pit as they follow the characters as they descend. Their movements create a slight glow in the dirt that characters have a 1-in-6 chance to notice unless they spend some time watching the walls (in which case they have a 3-in-6 chance). The movements of the coal demons also cause the dirt to bulge outward slightly. When the creatures surface, they try to knock characters off the platforms or out of their climbing gear.

If any characters are holding onto the walls (such as thieves climbing down the shaft), the coal demons push upward under the character's grip, burning their hands for 1d4 points of damage. The character must make a saving throw to keep their hold on the wall.

The coal demons leap across the pit to grab characters who are flying or floating down the shaft. These creatures are not afraid of falling as they simply catch the wall and burrow inward.

Coal Demons (6): HD 3; **HP** 20, 18, 15x2, 14, 10; **AC** 4[15]; **Atk** 2 fiery claws (1d4 + 1d4 fire); **Move** 12 (burrow 12); **Save** 14; **AL** C; **CL/XP** 3/60; **Special:** immune to fire. (see Appendix C: New Monsters)

Read the following once characters reach the bottom of the pit:

The warm, muggy air down here smells mildly of mildew, dirt, and dust. A tunnel opens to the east. Following it for a short distance, you see bits of roof shale and painted stone embedded in the walls, ceiling, and floor of the otherwise natural stone and dirt tunnel.

The roof shale and painted stone are very unusual to find in mines or caverns. These pieces come from Nuwa's palace and the other Heavenly buildings that fell during the collapse of the four pillars. Dwarves notice that the characters are definitely descending into the earth.

A foul stench of rot and feces wafts to your nostrils.

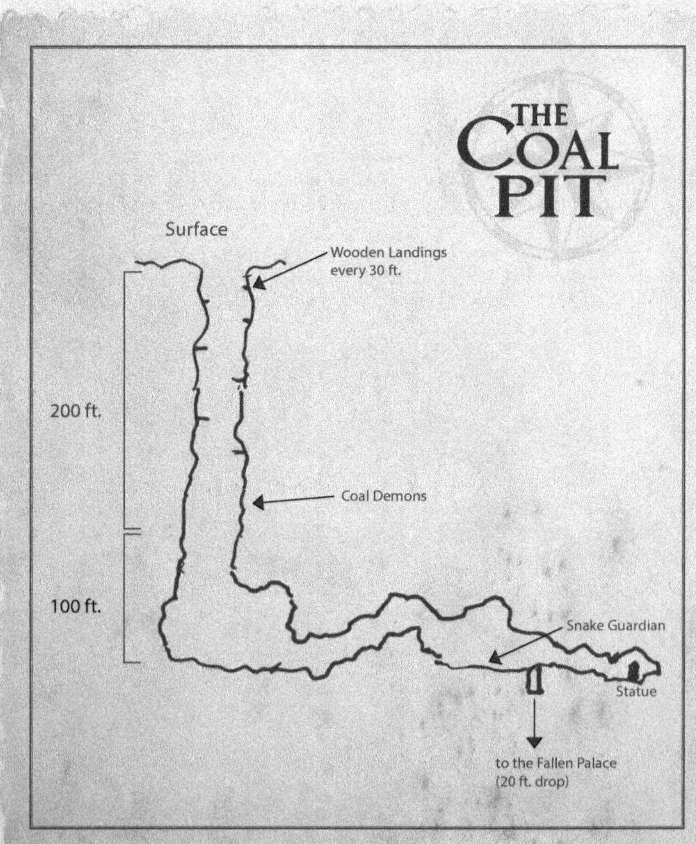

Give the characters some time to react, prepare, and maybe even get the jump on the snake ahead.

> Cresting a rise in the tunnel, you see nearly a dozen dead, decaying miners. Two piles of bones are picked clean and discarded along one side of this tunnel. A single hiss is followed by another, and another, until a chorus rings out.
>
> A massive, seven-headed snake slithers out of the shadows. Dried black ichor crusts the corner of its many red eyes. Festering wounds expose a number of ribs along the snake's body. Much of its midsection festers with abscesses.

Once a guardian of Nuwa's palace, this **fallen seven-headed snake guardian** fell into the depths of the underworld with the palace and was corrupted. The snake doesn't have any treasure.

Fallen Seven-Headed Snake Guardian: HD 10; **HP** 71; **AC** 2[17]; **Atk** 7 bites (1d8 + poison); **Move** 15; **Save** 5; **AL** C; **CL/XP** 12/2000; **Special: +1 or better magic weapons to hit,** poison, swallow whole (natural 20 to hit, automatic 1d8 damage per round). (see Appendix C: New Monsters)

If the fallen guardian is defeated, the characters can discover a 20-foot-deep hole in the tunnel floor. The hole is more than five feet in diameter and worn smooth from the snake traveling in and out. If the characters continue exploring the tunnel before they drop down, they quickly find that it dead-ends at a crumpled wall near the remains of a statue.

The statue was once two snake tails intertwined with the upper bodies of a man and a woman facing each other. Now, it is split down the middle with the man and woman falling to opposite sides. The arms and parts of their heads are shattered, and large portions of the tail disappear into the cavern and crumpled wall.

Characters who drop down the hole land on the rooftop of the worship hall (**Area 10**). A nest with five four-foot-tall eggs is on this rooftop. Three are intact but two are only broken shells. These eggs were laid hundreds of years ago.

Cultist Entrance

> It isn't hard to spot where the cliff folds in on itself to form a "V" shape in the rock. It's hard to believe this is the entrance to some "great temple."

Searching the surface of the rock wall reveals a small, one-inch-diameter indentation where a chop could fit. Mei Lan installed this magical doorway for the cultists to travel to and from Nuwa's Fallen Palace. Every supplicant must wear his or her chop in order to pass through the doorway.

> Slipping in the chop, the lock begins to turn clockwise and rotates until it stops with a click. Light blue lines crackle like veins across the stone, and a gentle gust of air pushes outward. The blue lines grow and become an oval portal with colors shimmering across the surface like light passing through a piece of quartz.

This portal radiates magic. Characters cannot see what is on the other side. Characters who step through find themselves outside the wing entrance (**Area B-1**) of Nuwa's Fallen Palace.

Area B: Nuwa's Fallen Palace

B-1. Wing Entrance

If the characters use the cultists' keys to enter, they are dimensionally teleported here.

> You find yourselves in front of a subterranean castle, in a huge cavern. The castle appears to be somewhat damaged, and in some places it melds into the rock — you get the sense that it was not originally built underground, but somehow merged into this oppressive place as a result of magic or some bizarre catastrophe. Nevertheless, it is vast, and if this is only a portion of the original you cannot conceive how large it must have once been.
>
> You stand outside a large red double door. A pillar on each side of the door is formed of a coiled giant snake spiraling its way to the top. The snake's maw is open, and the fangs bite into the underside of the awning. The building itself is old and worn. There's evidence of significant damage, with cracks running up the foundation into the lower half of the walls. Broken shingles from the roof are strewn on the ground.

B2. through B6. Servants' Quarters

These five rooms share the same general description with only a few minor changes.

> This room obviously once served as quarters for the palace servants. Cracked and timeworn murals of dancing and feasts cover the walls. A closer look reveals that the participants all have human upper bodies but the lower bodies of snakes.
>
> The original furniture has been stripped save for an ancient metal latrine basin in the corner. In their place are straw mat cots wrapped in linen. Small bundles sit at the foot of each of the beds. A coal-dusted white linen partition provides a modicum of privacy between each roommate.

The bundles at the foot of each bed include a change of clothes, an empty rice bowl, chopsticks, and a concealed weapon harness. The clothes belong to the cultists. Characters may use them as disguises if they desire. Characters also find six whetstones in the room.

A sketchbook someone has secretly been keeping is hidden under a floorboard beneath a cot in one of the rooms. All the art is drawn with coal dust, and most depict the same three people. The two men and one woman all appear to be in their late 20s to early 30s. Most of the pieces depict them fishing or down by the river. One stands out from the rest and shows the three sitting down for a tea ceremony.

Stuffed into one of the straw cots is a handful of miscellaneous jade jewelry.

Read the following when characters leave the second room:

> As you begin to leave the room, giggles fill the air around you, but you don't see anyone. Finally the giggling subsides and a voice speaks up, "And where are you running off to in such a hurry?" With these words, the white linen curtains pull from their anchors and dance around the room. The swirling fabric advances quickly and whirls around, obscuring sight. The walls disappear and the world spins.

The enchanted linens are actually created by *phantasmal force* spells cast by the **4 underworld phantasms** found in the room. The fabric dance for another round before they fall to the ground, where they form into fashionable robes draped over a dozen beautiful men and women (also part of the *phantasmal force*).

Nuwa's Fallen Palace

The small, dark, confined space disappears, replaced by a brightly lit and opulent banquet hall filled with music, food, and drink. Several beautiful men and women with food and drink in hand rush up to you. Silk panels lining the walls depict painted portraits of people dressed in reds and blues with trims of gold. Beautiful trees and gardens are painted onto other silk panels. A final set of panels has a poem about the kindness and generosity of their creator. It feels as if you have stepped into the murals on the walls of the rooms, except these people definitely have legs and not snake tails.

The illusionary men and women ply the characters with kindness, food, drink, and promise their heart's desires. After casting their illusions about the room, the phantasms cast *charm person* on a couple of characters, hoping to turn them against their comrades. Characters who maintain their wits are attacked. If a fight begins, the jovial scene around the characters darkens, and the majority of the people in the room simply fade away, leaving just the four undead phantasms.

Underworld Phantasms (4): HD 5; HP 38, 35, 34, 29; **AC** 5[14]; **Atk** ghostly touch (1d6); **Move** 12 (fly); **Save** 12; **AL** C; **CL/XP** 7/600; **Special:** +1 or better magic weapons to hit, spell-like abilities, wail (3/day, 20ft radius, 2d6 damage, save for half).
Spell-like abilities: 3/day—charm person, darkness 15ft radius, phantasmal force.

B-7. INNER DOOR

This is the inner door of the palace wing and separates the servants' quarters from Nuwa's inner sanctum. The walls on either side of this door are painted with murals of a snake-bodied creature with a human torso and head. The being is defeating a variety of monsters. The snake's body moves across several scenes, weaving between the monsters. The mural is in disrepair from age and the fall from Heaven.

B-8. OUTER COURTYARD

Some of the black metal cages (equivalent to cold iron) hanging over the courtyard detect of magic. A large pile of ash is off to one corner of the courtyard. Investigating it reveals small remnants of furniture. The cultists piled rotting and broken furniture from various rooms here and burned the heap.

Characters searching for the whimpering soul find a white fox named *Bi³Shou³* (Bishou, "Monarch's Hand") in one of the square cages. The fox is wounded and weak. A strange crank is on the outside of the magical cage, but nothing is visible that should stop the fox from squeezing between the bars.

This crank was used to shrink the cage, which forced Bishou to shift from his human form to that of the fox. The handle can be cranked in the opposite direction to make the cage up to three times bigger, which is enough space for a human.

Bishou can also be written to mean Sheltering Hand (Protector) but it would still be pronounced exactly the same in verbal communication. Bishou works for Lord Wu² (Wu, "Nobody"), the gatekeeper of Heaven. He was sent to retrieve the soul gourd and deliver it to the Eternal Vault. Both interpretations of Bishou's name speak to his station.

Bishou can speak while in animal form, but he currently has large blanks in his memory. He feels as if his memory is actively slipping away while he talks with the characters. He's been focusing on remembering his mission to retrieve something belonging to his lord. Yet he cannot remember his lord's name or the item.

He knows that the mission is very important and that the fate of many souls is on the line. He knows that many humans have come and gone while he has been in the cage. Recently, all but one of them left.

The cage leaches Bishou's magical powers and creates a feedback field that prevents him from teleporting out or squeezing between the bars. Bishou's Heavenly soldier nature is directly oppositional to the place in which he's being kept, so it is slowly draining away his self-identity and his memories.

Characters can also pick the lock of the cage to release Bishou. The magic doesn't prevent tampering from the outside of the cage.

Bishou has a sandy-colored birthmark shaped like a gourd just below his neck on the front of his chest. The blood of mortals, including the blood in this courtyard, burns the white fox on contact and lights his fur on fire. The divine fox burns until the fire is put out and the blood is washed off (the fire won't kill him, although it pains him greatly). He is still appreciative of the characters for dousing the flames if they do so.

Bishou, Divine Fox Warrior: HD 6; **HP** 41; **AC** 2[17]; **Atk** bite (1d4 + 1d6 electricity) (fox form only) or weapon (1d8 + 1d6 electricity) (human form only); **Move** 12; **Save** 11; **AL** L; **CL/XP** 9/1100; **Special:** +1 or better magic or silver weapons to hit, immune to electricity and fire, lightning bolt (3/day, 2d6 damage, save for half), magic resistance (15%), shape change (at will into white fox), spell-like abilities.
Spell-like abilities: at will—cure light wounds, fly, haste, light, protection from evil; 1/day—teleport.

Two of the cages house miners from the search party that was sent after the first group of miners who went missing. They are dehydrated and starving but can be healed and questioned. Their cages have inward-facing spikes along the walls and roofs. Their names are *Tu³An¹* (Tuan, "Peaceful Earth") and *Gu³Dong⁴* (Gudong, "Drum in Motion"). Both miners beg the characters to release them from the cages and take them back to Mei Zhen.

Tuan saw other prisoners taken away, never to return. But the cultists stopped taking people days, maybe weeks, ago. He doesn't have an exact count of days because there's no real sense of time down here. He doesn't know why they stopped, but he's certain the reprieve won't last forever.

They've seen the cultists come and go and believe their leader is someone named Fei Du. They've only seen her once or twice, but she mentioned that her patron ordered the feedings be put on hold. They don't know what that means.

Gudong recalls that a group of cultists came through recently. They carried bloody weapons and took a girl into the big two-story building. They exited without their weapons and the girl. He thinks he passed out for a while but remembers waking up later when all the cultists were leaving.

Gudong hasn't seen Fei Du since that day, so he guesses she left with the cultists.

Another cage has earth and fire sprites packed tightly together. They're weak but when the characters approach, they stomp and buzz about trying to communicate. The cage radiates magic, and the sprites bounce against some sort of forcefield between the bars. Characters cannot communicate with them unless they share an elemental language or have some magical means to do so. The cultists captured the sprites, and the cult leader was "eating" them by sucking their souls into a magical gourd and then drinking the soul from the gourd. She recently stopped, but they don't know why.

At some point while the characters are investigating the cages, the fresh blood pools rise up as **2 blood golems** and attack. These creatures are formed from the corruption in the area combined with Mei Lan's powers.

Hua Yue is not in any of the cages.

Blood Golems (2): HD 6; **HP** 42, 38; **AC** 3[16]; **Atk** 2 strikes (1d8 + blood consumption); **Move** 12; **Save** 11; **AL** N; **CL/XP** 9/1100; **Special:** +1 or better weapons to hit, blood consumption (gains hp equal to damage dealt), cell division (if enough blood is absorbed to take to maximum hp, splits into two identical golems with half current hit points), immune to mind-affecting abilities, regenerate (2hp/round), resist fire (50% damage), vulnerable to cold (slowed for 1d4 rounds). (see **Appendix C: New Monsters**)

B-9. Fei Du's Sanctum

Whatever this room once was, it has been transformed into a luxurious bedroom. White lanterns and a handful of candles provide light but also fill areas of the room with dancing shadows.

A sickly sweet perfume hangs oppressively in the air, mixed with the spicy scent of cinnamon and lightly musty machilus wood. There are polished redwood tables, stools, a bed, and a vanity, all engraved and carved with intricate designs of various winged creatures. Red, silk-covered pillows and sheets are embroidered with similar winged creatures in gold, white, and blue thread.

A woman sits cross-legged on the floor in front of a scholar's desk. She has pale skin marred by black veins that pulse up her neck and face. Her eyes are flooded with blood. She's gracefully holding one sleeve back and writing in an open scroll. She slides a well-manicured index finger up her brush and gestures for you to wait. She writes one more word and leans down to blow a greenish-gray breath across the paper before rolling the scroll closed.

Fei Du is in the process of losing her soul and transforming into a monster. She is currently penning the saga of her rise to immortality and godhood. She is egotistical and delusional. She believes she's ascending, when in reality all her experiments and practices have caused her to twist and mutate into a poisonous mogui.

If the characters play to her ego, she offers them tea and tells them her story, expecting to gain more worshippers. Unbeknownst to Fei Du, her fingernails are envenomed. Measuring the tea leaves infuses them with poison. Characters who drink the tea must make a saving throw vs. poison. If they fail, black veins spread across their skin and start choking them to death.

See the adventure background for details about her history.

Fei Du will answer a few questions:

- -Hua Yue is still alive. "That little thief stole a heart that doesn't belong to her. Now she's going to give back his gift if it's the last thing she does. My goddess will see to that and reward me for my service while punishing his betrayal."

- She believes she will ascend to take over for Niu Tian Shen once he's removed from the picture. Niu Tian Shen didn't understand his place, so he doesn't deserve to keep it.

Characters may circumvent this fight by turning Fei Du against her patron goddess. If she can be convinced that Mei Lan is not going to hold up her end of the deal, she joins the characters in confronting the goddess.

Fei Du wears expensive green robes embroidered all over with winged creatures. Half her hair is pinned up with several jade, gold, and pearl accessories. The black veins spreading across her skin and her long green fingernails contrast sharply with her pale features.

If a fight begins, Fei Du flings her robes out to create a poisonous cloud to affect as many characters as possible. She fights with two poisoned daggers, gaining a +2 to-hit bonus thanks to her gown hiding her attacks. She can also throw the daggers with the +2 to-hit bonus, and the daggers return to her hand. She enjoys jumping supernaturally high and striking at her opponents from the air. She then lands outside their melee reach. Characters struck by her daggers or claws must make a saving vs. her poison or die.

Fei Du, Unseelie Fey Mogui: HD 10; **HP** 74; **AC** 3[16]; **Atk** 2 claws (1d6 + poison) or 2 daggers (1d4+1 + poison); **Move** 12 (30ft leap); **Save** 5; **AL** C; **CL/XP** 12/2000; **Special:** +1 or better magic weapons to hit, leap (30ft leap), poison (save or die), poison cloud (3/day, 30ft diameter, save or choke for 1d6+4 rounds), spell-like abilities
Spell-like ability: at will—*faerie fire, locate animals*; 3/day—*cure light wounds, heat metal*.
Equipment: *+1 throwing dagger that returns to the hand* (x2), jade, gold, and pearl hair accessories (200 gp).

Once characters deal with Fei Du, they have free rein to search her room. A redwood altar box with orchids carved into its ivory door panels is in a dark corner on the opposite side of the room from the bed. Wisps of incense float from the negative spaces between the carvings. (Ivory is extremely rare because of the region's Taoist and Buddhist culture. Sourcing ivory would normally be from an animal that died of natural causes.)

Characters who open the box find:

- Several wooden panels painted with various colors of orchid flowers.
- A gold statue of a beautiful woman dressed in long flowing robes standing on an open orchid flower. Her robes are engraved with orchids that are filled in with colored dyes.
- An offering of peaches and oranges in a jade bowl with two dragons carved on opposite sides. The lip of the bowl is so thin that light passes through it. Characters who eat the offerings bring bad luck on themselves. They are forced to reroll a single successful die roll and keep the new result before the end of the adventure.

A gold incense bowl in the room is filled with sand and holds three sticks of still-burning incense. It's clear that this is where the strong smell of cinnamon and machilus wood is coming from.

A secret compartment in the bed contains the *soul gourd* the white fox Bishou was sent to retrieve. The *soul gourd* detects of powerful magic (see **Appendix B: New Items**).

The mirror on the vanity shows each character not as they look but as they wish to see themselves. It was a gift to Fei Du from Mei Lan so she wouldn't see what she was actually becoming.

Inside the drawers of the vanity, characters find jewelry and some makeup. Included in the jewelry is a complicated decorative knot linked with three coins. It radiates magic and absorbs 1d4 x 10 points of damage inflicted on the wielder before it unravels itself.

A sharpened hairpin functions as a +1 freezing dart that returns to the hand.

B-10. Worship Hall

This room is two stories tall with the second story being an internal balcony with staircases leading up from two sides. An eight-foot-tall wooden statue in the center of the far wall is of the same beautiful woman as found in the altar box in Fei Du's sanctum (**Area B-9**), complete with her standing on an orchid. The flooring appears to be made of some sort of packed clay. Otherwise, the room is empty.

Characters who go upstairs find that the stairs are rickety and not maintained. Boards may break off. Characters who successfully make it to the top find themselves breaking through brittle and weak flooring. The wood is infested with the same blight as the furniture that the cultists piled up and burned. Characters have a 20% chance of falling through the floor and taking 1d6 points of damage.

B-11. Mess Hall

This room is mostly empty, with only some straw mats covered in linen left for seating around the room. Characters can find a large bucket containing empty bowls, several jars of fermented food items, and a bamboo box filled with cold, cooked rice.

B-12. and B-13. Collapsed Buildings and Inner Courtyard

This area is pitch black. Characters must provide their own light sources or have darkvision to compensate.

These aren't statues. They are actually underworld creatures in stasis caused by the magical fallout when the palace fell from Heaven. Mei Lan's ritual is waking them.

When the characters reach the middle of the inner courtyard, they start to hear the rumbling of earth and feel minor tremors in the ground beneath their feet. The creatures are pulling themselves free.

The **2 blue-skinned devils** come to life and attack.
Blue-Skinned Devil (Mogui) (2): HD 7; **HP** 51, 47; **AC** 4[15]; **Atk** 4 claws (1d6) or gore (2d8); **Move** 15; **Save** 9; **AL** C; **CL/XP** 9/1100; **Special:** +1 or better magic weapons to hit, burst of speed (1/day, double movement), additional 1d8 damage to gore attack), cone of fire (1/day, 60ft cone, 8d6 damage, save for half), stasis (remain motionless, cannot be harmed). (see **Appendix C: New Monsters**)

B-14. Nuwa's Fallen Sanctum

This is where Nuwa stored her cache of color-stones.

The woman on the throne is **Mei Lan**, while **Hua Yue** sits on the floor. If the characters attack Mei Lan, Hua Yue throws herself in the way and calls out to the group. She claims that Mei Lan is just trying to save her husband.

Hua Yue is under the effects of a *charm person* spell cast by Mei Lan. This causes Hua Yue to believe Mei Lan is her trusted best friend and behaves accordingly. It is important to understand that Hua Yue's nature and motivations are still accessible to the characters.

Hua Yue, Female Human: HP 4; **AC** 9[10]; **Atk** none; **Move** 12; **Save** 18; **AL** L; **CL/XP** B/10; **Special:** none. (**Monstrosities** 254)

Mei Lan is not completely evil, yet. She is lovesick and her perspective on the world has been warped with time and her powers. If she isn't set on a different course soon, Leigong or another Heavenly soldier is likely to be sent to remove her from existence.

She has no interest in fighting the characters. She has convinced Hua Yue that she must return the xiao to Niu Tian Shen so that he can be healed and made whole.

If Fei Du is with the characters, she accuses Mei Lan of tricking and using her. She is quite open about her version of what happened. She has done everything Mei Lan asked of her, including pausing her experiments on the prisoners.

In the hands of the rightful owner, the xiao can summon Niu Tian Shen. If this happens, Mei Lan has medicine prepared to heal him once he's made whole. Secretly, Mei Lan also intends to dose her husband with a cup of Meng Po's five-flavored tea of forgetfulness for a fresh start to their relationship.

Meng Po

Meng Po is the goddess of the afterlife. She serves a special soup on the Bridge of Forgetfulness to wipe a person's memory before they step into the afterlife or are reincarnated. She waits for dead souls at the entrance to the ninth realm of the dead.

Alternatively, she is known for collecting various herbs from earthly ponds and streams to make her five-flavored tea of forgetfulness. This tea is given to each soul to drink before they leave the underworld. The tea causes immediate and permanent amnesia as it wipes away all memories of their past lives.

Mei Lan and Niu Tian Shen were married through an arranged marriage. She fell madly in love with Niu Tian Shen, while he eventually grew to love her. Still, they struggled to get along; it was a volatile relationship with poor communication. Eventually, the two agreed to live separate lives. Since then, Niu Tian Shen has avoided the mountains where his wife resides.

If asked about her association with the cultists, she expresses embarrassment. "I let jealousy get the best of me, I'll admit."

Mei Lan claims that the cultists were doing some very evil things before she came around. She put a stop to it and was helping them seek redemption. She actually did stop the cultists from continuing their murder spree, which is something hinted at by prisoners in the outer courtyard (**Area B-8**). Mei Lan figured that if she couldn't redeem Fei Du and the cultists, she would turn them over for judgement.

Characters can point out that she used her knowledge and powers to cause harm to humans and spirits. She initially denies this, but can be persuaded to see the truth. The characters' best bet is to reason with the quasi-deity, as she is a tough opponent. She is not truly evil, and characters who appeal to her better nature can turn her away from the destructive path she is currently on.

Arcane and divine characters may notice during the conversation that the crystals seem to be activated for some sort of siphoning ritual. If confronted about this, Mei Lan explains that she was trying to save her husband's essence because she didn't know how else to retrieve his horn or summon him.

However, characters may very likely attack her on sight. This would be a difficult fight, but if they use zhenniao feathers from the provincial roadhouse to concoct their own dose of poison, they can use it against Mei Lan. If she fails her saving throw, she has a 20% chance of failing to cast any spell she attempts due to confusion caused by the toxin.

If Mei Lan drops below 40 hit points, she teleports away with a parting curse under her breath (if reduced suddenly to 0 hit points, assume that she has enough willpower left to escape). Characters earn her ire. She ends up somewhere gravely wounded and very peeved.

Mei Lan (Fey Deity): HD 14; **HP** 107; **AC** 1[18]; **Atk** charged strike (2d8 + 1d6 electricity); **Move** 15; **Save** 3; **AL** N; **CL/XP** 17/3500; **Special:** +2 or better magic weapons to hit, charm person (3/day, –2 save), immune to fire and cold, magic resistance (30%), regenerate (3hp/round), spell-like abilities.
Spell-like abilities: at will—*detect magic, ESP, magic missile, phantasmal force, sleep*; 3/day—*dimension door, hold person, invisibility, lightning bolt, mirror image*; 1/day—*teleport*; 1/week— *mass charm*.

Concluding the Adventure

After characters talk sense into Mei Lan or defeat her in combat, they can find a bloodstained knife that is being used to siphon Niu Tian Shen's lifeforce. The blade is embedded in a color-stone. Pulling the knife from the color-stone disrupts the ritual and returns Niu Tian Shen to normal (see below).

Hua Yue can summon Niu Tian Shen by playing the xiao. She's then able to return his horn, which fuses back into place.

Several options for concluding the adventure include but are not limited to:

Mei Lan and Niu Tian Shen are reunited

Niu Tian Shen is healed, but his memory has also been erased. Mei Lan uses this opportunity to build a new reality and a new beginning for them. Niu Tian Shen and Mei Lan renew their marital vows, and he moves into the mountains with her.

Unfortunately, this leaves Niu Tian Shen only tenuously tied to his domain. Agriculture in the region suffer for years, and the land won't be able to support the current population. A significant recession occurs.

If characters don't rescue Hua Yue, she disappears, never to be heard from again.

Niu Tian Shen is reunited with his true love, Hua Yue

Once Niu Tian Shen is made whole, characters can heal him with their magic. The lands are revitalized and heal before the night of Qixi.

Fei Du is set on a path of redemption

Fei Du is open to suggestions on how to redeem herself. If the characters don't direct her path, she seeks out Lord Wu and begs him to allow her to serve him in penance.

The characters walked away from the adventure or didn't finish before the night of Qixi

The lands continue to die. On the night of Qixi, Mei Lan's siphoning ritual consumes Niu Tian Shen's soul, which severs his connection with the land. She feeds him Meng Po's five-flavored tea of forgetfulness and takes him away to her home in the skies.

Within days, the lands start wasting away to desert. Fei Du rises as a dark lord of the land.

Names and phrases in Chinese often have multiple meanings because the spoken word can have multiple ways to write it; the different written characters have different meanings. This wordplay is used in this module with characters such as Fei Du, which means Flight and Read/Study, but written differently can mean Fragrant Poison. The following tables contains some common words and phrases you can use in the adventure, as well as the names and meanings of various NPCs.

NAMES

Name	Phonetic Writing	English
牛天神	Niu Tian Shen	Ox Lord of New Day's Toil
美蘭	Mei Lan	Beautiful Orchard
飛讀/翡毒	Fei Du	Flight & Study/Fragrant Poison
嬅月	Hua Yue	Tranquil Moon
毋	Wu	"Nobody" (Surname Form)
辟手/庇手	Bishou	Monarch's Hand/Sheltering Hand (Protector)
土安	Tuan	Peaceful Earth
鼓動	Gudong	Drum in Motion
煤鎮/梅鎮	Mei Zhen	Coal Town/Plum Flower Town
謂風	Weifeng	Reason's Wind
雷公	Leigong	God of Thunder
洋	Yang	Ocean, Vast, Silver Coin, Foreign

PHRASES

Chinese	Phonetic Writing	English
你好	Ni^3 Hao^3	Hello (informal)
您好	Nin^2 Hao^3	Hello (formal)
再見	Zai^{4}jian^4	Goodbye
謝謝	Xie^{4}xie	Thank you
不客氣	Bu^{4}ke^{4}qi	You're welcome
歡迎光臨	Huan^{1}ying^{2}guang^{1}lin^2	Welcome (in the context of hospitality)
走了	Zou^3 Le	Gone away (through movement)
多少錢	Duo^1 Shao^3 Qian^2	How much money?
來了	Lai^{2}le	Arriving/Coming!

Appendix B: New Items

Medium Miscellaneous Magical Item

Day of the Seven Cranes (book)

Characters who flip through this book see diagrams of motion and notes about focusing and channeling one's lifeforce to direct certain outcomes. Many of the poses and motions reflect the movements of a crane in flight and on land.

A monk character may study the martial practices within this manual for one week, excluding all activity other than eating, sleeping, and training. At the end of a week, the character gains a +1 Armor Class bonus due to the defensive maneuvers they learn. This armor class bonus fades if the character does not practice the training each day for at least one uninterrupted hour while using the manual as a reference. The manual can provide this bonus only to one creature at a time. If training is not performed for more than a week, a character must restart their one-week training with the book, or another character can begin their own study. Usable by monks.

Lesser Miscellaneous Magical Item

Hua Yue's Xiao

This is a vertical end-blown flute bearing a scene of a woman dancing her way to the mountains skillfully carved into the material. It is made from the horn of the deity Niu Tian Shen. When played, it casts a *phantasmal force* that last until the character stops playing.

Successfully playing the instrument during the adventure does two things:
- The flute manifests a vision based on the song played. If the characters play a sad ballad, they call forth a vision of the attack at the provincial roadhouse. Characters can manifest other visions when playing music, depending on the song. With time, the characters may even learn to control how the visions manifest.
- The music calms the maddened Niu Tian Shen. (This is important if characters track him down later in the adventure.)

Greater Miscellaneous Magical Item

Soul Gourd

The *soul gourd* is a powerful magical artifact created from a bottle gourd that can trap souls and allow them to be drunk as elixirs. The wielder of the gourd must be within 30 feet of a target to use the item. The target must make a saving throw with a +2 bonus to avoid having its soul torn from its body and trapped in the gourd. The target's body collapses in a comatose state.

Over the course of the next week, the gourd converts the trapped soul into a liquid. A soul stolen from a Lawful being tastes refreshing, while a Neutral soul is a bland beverage. A Chaotic being's soul is bitter and foul-tasting. If the stolen soul is "poured" over the target's original body before the week is up, the soul returns to the creature. Once the soul is fully converted, the original body dies and cannot be restored. The gourd can contain only one soul at a time.

The full gourd functions as a *beaker of potions* and allows the wielder to create 1d4 + 1 different potions of their choosing. Also, the imbiber is healed for 3d6 points of damage and becomes 1d8 years younger. However, the character must make a saving throw and becomes Chaotic. Each successive drink requires a new saving throw with a cumulative −1 penalty.

Bottle gourds have many magical and symbolic references, from being Taoist fulu charms to holding magical elixirs. Some myths even claim bottle gourds might be portals to other worlds.

Spirit Money

Spirit money is not technically a magic item, but it is a means of connecting with the spirit world.

Spirit money (also known as Hell money, incense paper, or joss paper) is burned for the dead or for mystical beings to ensure that they are well taken care of in the spirit world. Sometimes, objects fashioned out of this special paper — such as paper jewelry, clothes, or furniture — are burned as offerings.

Zhenniao Poison

Zhenniao are daemon birds with varied reports on their appearance. The most common stories describe them as a cross between a peacock and a crane. They are extremely poisonous, from beak to feather. Lore speaks of their venom coming from the poisonous vipers that make up the bulk of these unique birds' diets. The poison's interaction with the birds' chemistry concentrates and mutates the viper poison, infusing the birds from beak to tail feathers. One bite of their meat is said to cause instant death in a human.

While no known antidote or cure exists in the mortal world, lore speaks of neutralizing the toxin using a great rhino horn but only if the poison isn't yet in the bloodstream.

Appendix C: New Monsters

The following monsters appear in this adventure:

Blood Golems

Hit Dice: 6
Armor Class: 3[16]
Attack: 2 strikes (1d8 + blood consumption)
Special: Blood consumption, cell division, +1 or better weapon to hit, regenerate (2 hp/round), immune to mind-affecting abilities, resistant to fire (50%)
Move: 12
Saving Throw: 11
Alignment: Neutrality
Number Encountered: 1, 1d4
Challenge Level/XP: 9/1,100

This creature looks like a hideous, bloated slug, blood red in color. Two long spindly arms protrude from its upper body. It has no other discernible features. Contrary to their name, blood golems are not constructs, but rather slug-shaped clots of living blood animated by a dark and ancient ritual. A typical blood golem is 10 feet long and weighs 700 pounds.

Each time a blood golem hits a living opponent with an attack, it gains a number of hit points equal to the damage dealt. These bonus hit points are added to the blood golem's total. When a blood golem absorbs enough blood to raise its hit points to the maximum for its HD, it splits into two identical blood golems, each with half the original's hit points. For example, a 6 HD blood golem that reaches 48 hit points splits into two 6 HD blood golems with 24 hit points each.

A blood golem is *slowed* (as the spell) for 1d4 rounds by any cold-based attacks or effects. A *purify food and water* spell deals 1d6 points of damage per caster level to a blood golem. A blood golem can attempt a saving throw to reduce the damage by half.

Blood Golem: HD 6; AC 3[16]; Atk 2 strikes (1d8 + blood consumption); **Move** 12; **Save** 11; **AL** N; **CL/XP** 9/1100; **Special:** +1 or better weapons to hit, blood consumption (gains hp equal to damage dealt), cell division (if enough blood is absorbed to take to maximum hp, splits into two identical golems with half current hit points), immune to mind-affecting abilities, regenerate (2hp/round), resist fire (50% damage), vulnerable to cold (slowed for 1d4 rounds).

Canker Vines

Hit Dice: 5
Armor Class: 5[14]
Attacks: slam (1d8 + entangle)
Saving Throw: 12
Special: acid, entangle, sleep poison
Move: 0 (immobile)
Alignment: Neutrality
Number Encountered: 1d3 (subterranean) or 1d8 (aboveground)
Challenge Level/XP: 6/400

Canker vines grow around themselves and resemble woven rope. The vines feed on life and can sense living Chi. They attack only living creatures, never undead or objects. These vines tend to grow around 30 to 60 feet long when bundled together.

When attacking, the vines open and extend outward like many tendrils to completely engulf the target. A creature struck by the vines must make a saving throw or be entangled. Boils of black ichor along the lengths of each individual vine burst against the skin of the entangled creature, automatically dealing 1d6 points of damage per round. Ensnared creatures must also make a saving throw saving throw or fall asleep (as *sleep* spell) from the sedative-laced ichor.

Canker Vine: HD 5; AC 5[14]; Atk slam (1d8 + entangle); **Move** 0 (immobile); **Save** 12; **AL** N; **CL/XP** 6/400; **Special:** acid (automatic 1d6 damage to entangled targets), entangle (save or held), sleep (entangled targets save or sleep as spell).

Coal Demons

Hit Dice: 3
Armor Class: 4[15]
Attacks: 2 fiery claws (1d4 + 1d4 fire)
Saving Throw: 14
Special: immune to fire
Move: 12/12 (burrowing)
Alignment: Chaotic
Number Encountered: 1d6 or 2d8
Challenge Level/XP: 3/60

Coal demons are six- to nine-inch-tall creatures with a torso made from a chunk of coal. Other smaller lumps of coal serve as appendages. They look a lot like massive versions of various molecular structures and come in a number of shapes and compositions of chunks of coal and dirt. Coal demons often burst out of the ground to attack with their fiery claws.

Coal Demon: HD 3; AC 4[15]; Atk 2 fiery claws (1d4 + 1d4 fire); **Move** 12 (burrow 12); **Save** 14; **AL** C; **CL/XP** 3/60; **Special:** immune to fire.

Fallen Seven-Headed Snake Guardian

Hit Dice: 10
Armor Class: 2[17]
Attacks: 7 bites (1d8 + poison)
Saving Throw: 5
Special: +1 or better magic weapons to hit, poison, swallow whole
Move: 15
Alignment: Chaotic
Number Encountered: 1, 1d4
Challenge Level/XP: 12/2,000

This seven-headed snake was a guardian of humanity but the fall of Nuwa's palace into the underworld allowed darkness and corruption to seep into its very essence. The 30-foot-long snake strikes with seven vicious bites that deliver a deadly venom to creatures that fail a saving throw. If it rolls a natural 20 to hit, it swallows the victim whole. Swallowed creatures automatically take 1d8 points of damage each round. The snake likes to "ferment" its meals by letting its victims die slowly; it swallows them whole at a later date.

Fallen Seven-Headed Snake Guardian: HD 10; AC 2[17]; Atk 7 bites (1d8 + poison); **Move** 15; **Save** 5; **AL** C; **CL/XP** 12/2000; **Special:** +1 or better magic weapons to hit, poison, swallow whole (natural 20 to hit, automatic 1d8 damage per round).

Fetid Hand Swarm

Hit Dice: 5
Armor Class: 5[14]
Attacks: swarm (2d6 + curse)
Saving Throw: 12
Special: Curse, nauseating smell, resist edged weapons, vulnerable to fire
Move: 12/12 (climbing)
Alignment: Neutrality
Number Encountered: 1d6
Challenge Level/XP: 6/400

Fetid hand swarms are collectives of severed hands that form from rotting tree bark and insects. They often form in areas where tragedy has occurred as the blood of the innocent soaks into the land and is drawn into the roots of the plants and trees. These swarms of hands emit a foul odor that nauseates victims drawn into the crawling swarm (–1 to hit and saves for 10 minutes, save resists). Characters who take damage must make a saving throw or suffer a rotting curse that does 1d4 points of damage per hour until healed. Fetid hand swarms take half damage from edged weapons, but take double damage from fire.

Fetid Hand Swarm: HD 5; AC 5[14]; Atk swarm (2d6 + curse); **Move** 12 (climb 12); **Save** 12; **AL** N; **CL/XP** 6/400; **Special:** curse (save or slow rot, 1d4 damage per hour until healed), nauseating smell (save or sickened for 10 minutes, –1 to hit and saves), resist edged weapons (50% damage), vulnerable to fire (200% damage).

Mogui (Mogwai)

Mogui (mogwai) comes from "mo" meaning evil beings that mean mortals harm, and "gui" meaning deceased vengeful spirits. They would often be associated in modern translations as devils, demons, and undead, with a variety of abilities. Listed below are a few types of mogui found in this adventure:

Mogui, Blue-Skinned Devils

Hit Dice: 7
Armor Class: 4[15]
Attacks: 4 claws (1d6) or gore (2d8)
Saving Throw: 9
Special: +1 or better magic weapons to hit, burst of speed, cone of fire, stasis
Move: 15
Alignment: Chaotic
Number Encountered: 1, 1d2
Challenge Level/XP: 9/1,100

Blue-skinned devils are 16-foot-tall mogui with horns, tusks, and four arms. They attack with their four claws or gore with their massive horns. Once per day, the mogui can direct a 60-foot-long cone of fire at their enemies (8d6 points of damage, save for half). They can cast darkness 15-foot radius and *invisibility* at will. Once per day, they can take to their hands and feet to double their movement for a short burst of speed. If they travel in a straight line and gore an opponent at the end of this run, they deal an additional 1d8 points of damage to their attack and toss the creature 1d3 x 10 feet. A creature can make a saving throw to take half damage and to avoid being tossed. A thrown creature takes an additional 1d6 points of damage for every 10 feet it is thrown.

A blue-skinned devil can enter a form of stasis (similar to a gargoyle) and remain motionless but aware of its surroundings. It becomes as hard as rock and cannot be harmed while in this state. They are often mistaken for statues.

Blue-Skinned Devil (Mogui): HD 7; AC 4[15]; Atk 4 claws (1d6) or gore (2d8); Move 15; Save 9; AL C; CL/XP 9/1100; **Special:** +1 or better magic weapons to hit, burst of speed (1/day, double movement, additional 1d8 damage to gore attack), cone of fire (1/day, 60ft cone, 8d6 damage, save for half), stasis (remain motionless, cannot be harmed).

Mogui, Chi Thief

	Corporeal	Incorporeal
Hit Dice:	6	6
Armor Class:	5[14]	1[18]
Attacks:	2 claws (1d8 + level drain) or weapon (1d8)	incorporeal touch (1d6)
Saving Throw:	11	11
Special:	+1 or better magic weapons to hit, level drain, reform	+1 or better magic weapons to hit, possession
Move:	12	12 (flying)
Alignment:	Chaotic	Chaotic
Number Encountered:	1, 1d4	1
Challenge Level/XP:	8/800	8/800

A chi thief mogui is a rather common type of mogui, a spirit returned to the land of the living that straddles life and death. When forced to confront their reality, they steal the chi of others in an attempt to return fully to the world of the living. They return in the form they remember from the moments before their death, but their slack, pale skin reveals their undead state. The circumstances of their death — be it a stab wound, an injury, or some other occurrence — are always visible on their forms, despite the creature not appearing to recognize them.

A chi thief often goes about its life as if nothing is happening. However, if they realize the facts of their death, they fly into a rage and attack all living creatures around them. Wisps of energy begin to flow around their features and are drawn into their eyes and mouths. The chi thief attacks with its claws and any weapon it might have carried.

Three times per day, the chi thief can grab a target it strikes and attempt to breathe in the chi of the creature. The target must make a saving throw or lose a level. Magic weapons are required to hit a chi thief mogui.

If slain, a mogui reforms in 1d4 days. If the body of the chi thief is completely destroyed, the creature returns in a ghostly form that attempts to possess a living creature. The target of this possession must succeed on a saving throw to resist the attempt. If it fails, the chi thief's incorporeal form pours into the living body. The chi thief completely controls the creature it possesses, although the original creature's psyche still remains for the time being. The possessed creature can make a new saving throw each day with a cumulative –1 penalty to expel the spirit (so a –1 penalty one day after the initial possession; a –2 penalty after two days; and a –3 penalty on the third day). If the creature fails all of these saves, the chi thief assumes control and cannot be removed. Over the next few days, the subsumed body reshapes itself to appear as the chi thief's original form. If a *dispel evil* spell is cast on the creature before the three days pass, the chi thief must make a saving throw or be expelled from the creature.

Mogui, Chi Thief (Corporeal): HD 6; AC 5[14]; Atk 2 claws (1d8 + level drain) or weapon (1d8); Move 12; Save 11; AL C; CL/XP 8/800; **Special:** +1 or better magic weapons to hit, level drain (1 level, save avoids), reform (return after 1d4 days).

Mogui, Chi Thief (Incorporeal): HD 6; AC 1[18]; Atk incorporeal touch (1d6); Move 12 (flying); Save 11; AL C; CL/XP 8/800; **Special:** +1 or better magic weapons to hit, possession (save or possessed, new save each day with cumulative –1 penalty to expel spirit, consumed after three days).

Mogui, Rot and Fecundity

Hit Dice: 10
Armor Class: 2[17]
Attacks: 2 claws (1d8 + fungus rot)
Saving Throw: 5
Special: +1 or better magic weapons to hit, fungus rot, spell-like ability
Move: 12/12 (flying)
Alignment: Chaotic
Number Encountered: 1, 1d6
Challenge Level/XP: 12/2,000

The rot and fecundity mogui are humanoids with sunken skin and long, rotted nails. Their eyes are completely black, like those of a shark, and green and black lightning sparks around the orbs. Fungus grows from their beards or eyebrows.

The mogui shoots green and black lightning bolts from its fingertips. If these bolts strike, fungus rapidly grows to cover the target. If the mogui hits the fungus with another lightning bolt, spores are released to incapacitate creatures. The mogui flies at its enemies and swipes at them with its deadly fingernails, hoping to infect them with a wasting disease.

Rot and Fecundity Mogui: HD 10; AC 2[17]; Atk 2 claws (1d8 + fungus rot); Move 12 (fly 12); Save 5; AL C; CL/XP 12/2000; **Special:** +1 or better magic weapons to hit, fungus rot (1d6 damage per hour, save each hour avoids damage, cure disease to end ongoing damage), spell-like ability, spores (10ft cloud, save or sleep as spell). **Spell-like ability:** at will—lightning bolt (1d8 damage and fungus rot, save for half damage and avoid rot; if already affected by fungus rot, save or additional 1d4 damage and spores released).

Mogui, Unseelie Fey

Hit Dice: 10
Armor Class: 3[16]
Attacks: 2 claws (1d8 + poison) or 2 daggers (1d4 + poison)
Saving Throw: 5
Special: +1 or better magic weapons to hit, leap, poison, poison cloud, spell-like abilities
Move: 12
Alignment: Chaotic
Number Encountered: 1, 1d3
Challenge Level/XP: 12/2,000

An unseelie fey mogui appears as a woman dressed in expensive, flowing robes. Their fey nature shows in their bearing and the perfection of their skin — but it is marred by black veins that spread across their features. Their fingernails are green and long, and drip with a deadly poison. They use their robes to hide their movements, granting them a +2 to-hit bonus to attacks. The fey can leap high into the air. They use this to their advantage and throw their daggers from this height then land out of range of their opponents.

Three times per day, the fey can fling wide her robes to create a 30-foot-diameter poison cloud that swirls around her form. Any creatures in this cloud must make a saving throw or inhale the poison and fall to the ground choking and coughing for 1d6+4 rounds.

Unseelie Fey Mogui: HD 10; AC 3[16]; Atk 2 claws (1d6 + poison) or 2 daggers (1d4 + poison); **Move** 12 (30ft leap); **Save** 5; **AL** C; **CL/XP** 12/2000; **Special:** +1 or better magic weapons to hit, leap (30ft leap), poison (save or die), poison cloud (3/day, 30ft diameter, save or choke for 1d6+4 rounds), spell-like abilities

Spell-like ability: at will—*faerie fire, locate animals*; 3/day—*cure light wounds, heat metal.*

Niu Tian Shen

	Corporeal	Incorporeal
Hit Dice:	14 (105 hit points)	14 (105 hit points)
Armor Class:	2[17]	−1[20]
Attacks:	slam (3d8 + poison slobber)	slam (3d8 + poison slobber)
Saving Throw:	3	3
Special:	+1 or better magic weapons to hit, magic resistance (20%), poison slobber	+1 or better magic weapons to hit, incorporeal, magic resistance (20%), poison slobber
Move:	15	15 (flying)
Alignment:	Neutrality	Neutrality
Number Encountered:	1	1
Challenge Level/XP:	17/3,500	17/3,500

The local deity Niu Tian Shen, "Ox Lord of New Day's Toil," manifests as a large, grayish-green bull with one horn. Slobber and snot runs from the bull's nose and mouth. The bull deity slams opponents with his powerful horn, knocking them backward 10 feet if they fail a saving throw. The slobber dripping from the bull's mouth and nose is poisonous, and any creature struck by the beast must make a saving throw or be struck by a glob of snot. The slobber burns like acid, dealing 1d6 points of damage per round if the target fails a saving throw. The slobber can be washed off or eliminated with *neutralize poison*. The deity is resistant to magic (20%).

When first encountered in the adventure, Niu Tian Shen is unable to manifest in corporeal form due to the zhenniao poison affecting his mind, which leaves him running on primal instinct. The incorporeal bull takes half damage from weapons and can pass through objects.

Niu Tian Shen (Corporeal): HD 14; HP 105; AC 2[17]; **Atk** strike (3d8 + poison slobber); **Move** 15; **Save** 3; **AL** N; **CL/XP** 18/3800; **Special:** +1 or better magic weapons to hit, poison slobber (save or rot, 1d6 damage per round until washed off or healed), spell-like abilities.

Spell-like abilities: at will—detect evil, polymorph self, purify food and drink; 3/day—bless, cure disease, speak with animals; 1/day—neutralize poison, prayer.

Niu Tian Shen (Incorporeal): HD 14; HP 105; AC −1[20]; **Atk** strike (3d8 + poison slobber); **Move** 15; **Save** 3; **AL** N; **CL/XP** 17/3500; **Special:** +1 or better magic weapons to hit, incorporeal (half damage from weapons), poison slobber (save or rot, 1d6 damage per round until washed off or healed).

Underworld Phantasms

Hit Dice: 5
Armor Class: 5[14]
Attacks: Ghostly touch (1d6)
Saving Throw: 12
Special: +1 or better magic weapons to hit, spell-like abilities, wail
Move: 12 (flying)
Alignment: Chaotic
Number Encountered: 1, 1d4, 2d6
Challenge Level/XP: 7/600

Underworld phantasms are translucent spirits with pale and tortured features. Their hair flows loosely back, and their eyes are hollow. These incorporeal beings are condemned to wander the underworld. The phantasms attack with a spectral touch. Three times per day, they can unleash a powerful wail.

Underworld Phantasms: HD 5; AC 5[14]; **Atk** ghostly touch (1d6); **Move** 12 (fly); **Save** 12; **AL** C; **CL/XP** 7/600; **Special:** +1 or better magic weapons to hit, spell-like abilities, wail (3/day, 20ft radius, 2d6 damage, save for half).

Spell-like abilities: 3/day—charm person, darkness 15ft radius, phantasmal force.

Wrath Dragon

Hit Dice: 10–12
Armor Class: 2[17]
Attacks: 2 claws (1d8), bite (2d12)
Saving Throw: 5, 4, or 3
Special: Breathes holy fire, turn undead
Move: 9/24 (flying)
Alignment: Law
Number Encountered: 1d2, or a nest (2 adults, 2 young)
Challenge Level/XP: Challenge level = (hit points/4) + 2

A wrath dragon is 30 feet long and weighs about 30,000 pounds. It has a serpentine neck and glittering silver scales. They breathe holy fire in a cone-shape 90 feet long and roughly 30 feet wide at the base. Wrath dragons have a 75% chance of being able to talk; talking wrath dragons have a 50% chance of being able to cast spells as a 6th-level Cleric. They can turn undead as an 8th-level Cleric.

Wrath Dragon: HD 10–12; AC 2[17]; **Atk** 2 claws (1d8), bite (2d12); **Move** 9 (fly 24); **Save** 5, 4, 3; **AL** L; **CL/XP** Challenge level = (hit points/4) + 2; **Special:** breathes holy fire (90ft cone, save for half damage), spells (2/2/1/1), turn undead (as 8th-level cleric).

About the Author

Alice is a Chinese-American born and raised in the San Francisco Bay area of California. Both her parents fled from China to Taiwan at very young ages and later immigrated to America. Growing up the oldest of two children, Alice was taught to speak Mandarin at home and English outside the home. While at home, she listened to tapes and watched Chinese TV shows about Sun[1] Wu[4]kong[1] (The Monkey King), Feng[1] Shen[2] Bang[4] (Creation of the Gods/Investiture of the Gods), and many stories about magic and mythology from the Chinese culture. This imbued her with a strong passion for the genre and culture. She hopes to give a glimpse into the epic craziness of a world where gods and immortals constantly meddle and involve themselves in the everyday lives of mankind.

Alice has been a pen & paper gamer since the late '90s and is a true polygamer. Every genre and system she can get exposure to, she tries to experience. She tries to experience games of every genre and system, from the crunch-heavy Hero System to the system light Ghost Echo. She's played more than 200 games, and that number continues to climb. Alice is a host of the Babies with Knives podcast that focuses on teaching a variety of tabletop roleplaying games.

NECROMANCER
Games™

www.ingramcontent.com/pod-product-compliance
Lightning Source LLC
Chambersburg PA
CBHW041202100726

47911CB00016B/827